A Woman in Pink

Megan A. Schikora

Regal House Publishing

Published by
Regal House Publishing, LLC
Raleigh, NC 27605

ISBN -13 (paperback): 9781646036936
ISBN -13 (epub): 9781646036943
Library of Congress Control Number: 2025937275

Cover images and design by © studiochi.art
Author photo by © Lauren Giuliani.

The following is a work of fiction created by the author. All names, individuals, characters, places, items, brands, events, etc. were either the product of the author or were used fictitiously. Any name, place, event, person, brand, or item, current or past, is entirely coincidental.

Printed in the United States of America

Regal House Publishing, LLC
https://regalhousepublishing.com

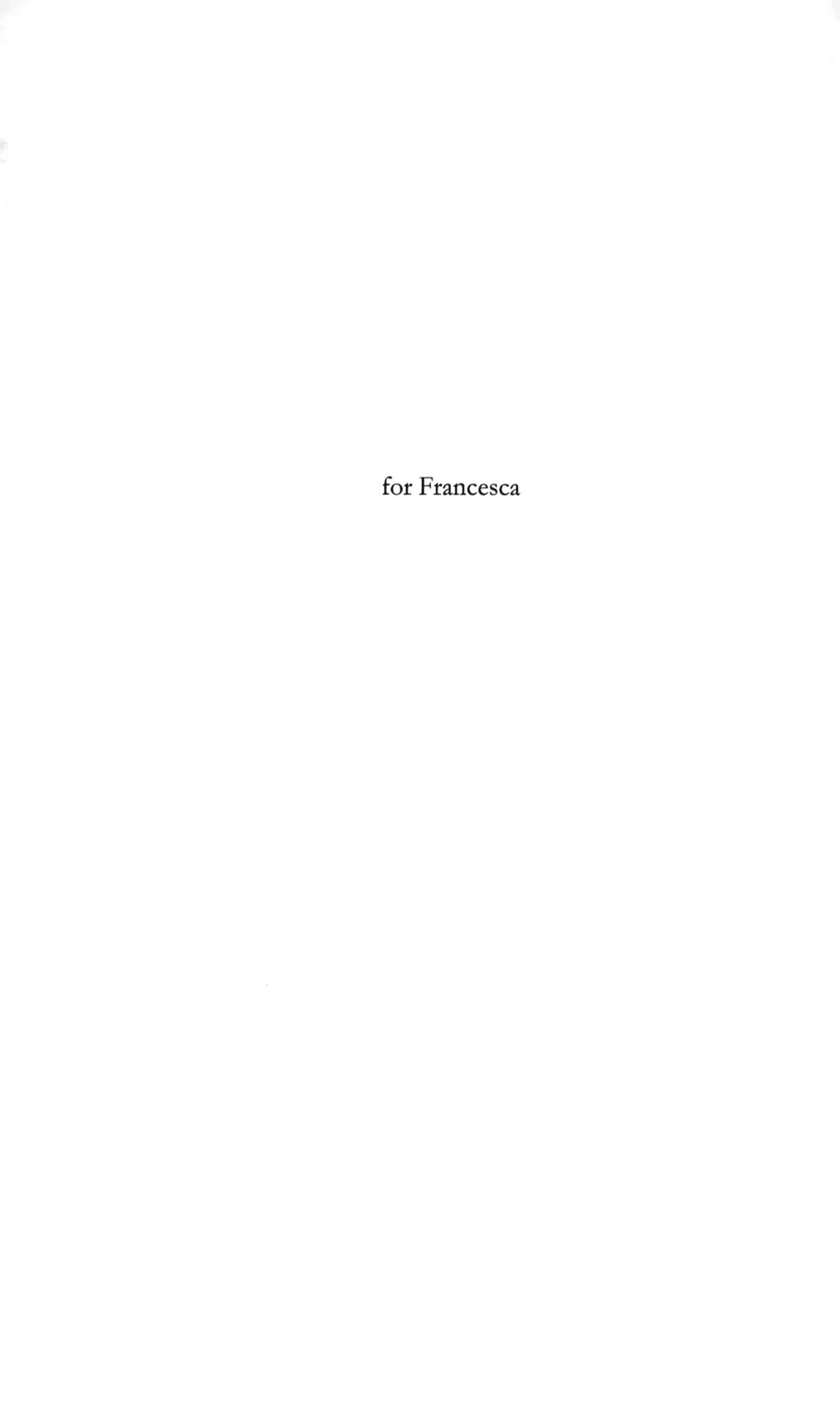

for Francesca

He taught me to love him, he called me his flower
That blossomed for him all the brighter each hour
But I awoke from my dreaming, my idol was clay
My visions of love have all faded away

—June Carter Cash, "Wildwood Flower"

1

Dear Sir or Madam:

I am writing on behalf of Dutch Van Lokeren, whom I've known for fifteen years. We met when we were twenty-nine.

I never saw him coming.

The night Dutch and I met, I was sitting cross-legged on my couch, a stack of student research papers fanned out beside me, when a text message from Kevin popped up: *At Hurley's. Wanna come up?* My twenties so far were strewn with Kevins—sweet, chivalrous guys who came from families like mine, in which men loved women in a distinctly 1950s way. Their code of conduct included always holding the door for a woman, paying her way, and walking her home. Their sexism was almost quaint. They would never trust a woman to change a tire or hold office, but they would never raise their voice or hand to one.

When I realized I'd become a woman who expected men to hold the door, pay my way, and walk me home, I wondered aloud to my girlfriends, "Am I sexist?"

But when they came to me with their troubles, tales of boyfriends who cheated on them and called them names and made them cry, I felt an uneasy, private appreciation for my upbringing. I'd dated good men who wanted confirmation that I'd arrived safely home at night, who kissed me only after they'd blushingly asked permission, who waited and waffled as they worked up the courage to ask for a real first date.

In the meantime, they operated like Kevin, testing the water by suggesting meetings like this, as if we were coworkers who might find ourselves at the same bar, and might as well chat over a drink.

My eyes and neck hurt from grading papers. I blandly regarded Kevin's message and thought, like when I received postcards from my dentist reminding me to make an appointment, *I should probably do this.* I tapped out a response: *Be up in a bit.*

Hurley's swelled that night, standing room only. I found Kevin at the bar, in conversation with Nick Gliston, a regular whom everyone called Glick, and Clever, the bartender.

He set two drinks in front of Kevin and Glick. "I call this the Skull Fuck. It'll change your lives." He looked hopefully at me. "You want one?"

I eyed the blue concoctions. "I think I'll stick with beer."

Looking forlorn, he brought me a Budweiser. He and Glick resumed their argument about some athlete's new multimillion-dollar contract.

I heard Dutch before I saw him. A rumbling baritone cut through the din, causing me to look down the length of the crowded bar. He was sitting at the end with a woman I couldn't immediately place. Then I realized she was a server there, wearing a tight pink sweater instead of her customary Hurley's polo shirt.

"I know him," Kevin said. Leaving Glick and Clever to their debate, we headed over to say hello. Kevin and Dutch were the kind of friends who had never exchanged phone numbers or made plans, but who spent so much time at Hurley's that they inevitably fell into conversation at regular intervals.

Dutch stood when we approached, towering over us, and the four of us fell into an easy rhythm of banter. He hadn't seen me before. My first time here? No, no, I'd done plenty of damage here. His was the only tan one in a sea of pasty winter faces. Where had he been? Florida, golf trip. How did everyone know each other?

As we chatted, he seemed to be standing in the sun's full dazzling force. And with his attention focused on me, I suddenly stood in it too.

He gestured at Kevin and me. "Are you guys together?"

"We're just hanging out," came my quick response. "How about you two?"

"We went out a few times." He smiled at the server like an

encouraging parent. "Decided we're better as friends though, right?"

The server's smile turned to acid.

As Dutch and I became more absorbed in our own conversation, I felt Kevin's rustling rancor and watched the server's face freeze into a mask. When Dutch asked me out in front of them, she looked like she'd been struck.

"Are you serious?" Kevin angled his body toward Dutch, his face incredulous. "You've got some fucking nerve."

It thrilled me. I gave Dutch my number.

The next night at dinner, the air between us popped and snapped. We moved to a bar down the street, our chatter a laughing, animated flurry, and he caught my hand. In the back entrance, a dim, unused stairwell that smelled vaguely of mildewed beer taps, he suddenly stopped me and pressed me to the dark wood paneling, his mouth on mine.

He drew back and tucked an errant lock of hair behind my ear, his voice uneven and gravelly. "Is there anyone else?"

"No."

"Will you say it?"

I could hardly form the words. "There's no one else."

To apply the full length of my body to his own and find my mouth again, he had to bend down and tighten the slack of his arms. What a wonder, I thought as I tilted my face up to his, to feel so small.

Like exuberant teenagers, we rushed into each other's physical and mental space, crowding it, welcoming it.

One afternoon I bounded through his front door and found him on his couch, engrossed in a NASCAR race on TV. My eyes narrowed with feigned suspicion. "Not really."

"Yes, really," he declared. "The first time I ever went, I took my snow cone all the way down to the fence, as close as I could get. First lap, the cars blew by me and blew that snow cone to fuckin' bits. I wasn't even sure I still had a face. And that's when I fell in love."

I laughed. "Never hung with a NASCAR guy before."

"I'll open up a whole new world for you." He grinned. "Next time I go to a race, I'll bring you and we'll get all the gear, head-to-toe American flags and motor-oil logos. Then we'll hit a poetry reading for you."

"Would you consider taking your gear off before we go to the reading?"

"Absolutely not. And neither can you."

Perhaps we were, at first glance, an incongruous pair, the constant drone of ESPN in his living room, of CNN in mine, my blue nail polish and clutter of bracelets, his jockish preppiness. But our conversations had a liquidity, a warm rushing current, an immediate intimacy, a series of clicks of perfect recognition. *Oh. It's you.*

We talked through the night in torrents. "Where have you *been*?" I asked repeatedly, as if joking.

His response was always the same. "Where have *you* been?"

I was sure, now that I knew him, that I would never again feel oceanic loneliness.

On my way home after parting, I would think of a dozen things I'd forgotten to tell him. And when I pulled out my phone to call him, it was ringing, him on the other end. We never stopped talking.

I wanted him near me, touching me, inside me, all the time. His proximity made me crackle. That I could be both perfectly understood and completely electrified by one person astounded me.

When we told each other our stories, they were different but the same, and when we agreed or disagreed, we did so with equal fervor, and the more we wound ourselves around each other, the more I wondered at it. *Oh. It's you.*

We talked endlessly about our families. He was an only child.

"Me too," I said. "But I never felt like one because my cousins were always around."

"How many cousins?"

I did a quick mental tally. "Forty."

"Forty?" He laughed. "Jesus."

"Jesus, yes. He needs us Irish Catholics to keep filling the ranks." I laughed with him. "We're formidable breeders."

"And you? Is your biological clock hammering away?"

"I hate that phrase," I said immediately. "It never comes out of my mouth."

"Women use that phrase all the time," he protested.

"I don't." I was adamant. "The whole 'biological clock' thing is just a hostage situation for women. We don't need that pressure."

"Fair enough. I won't use it anymore." He began again. "Do you think you want kids?"

"I don't know." I scrunched my face, remembering. "I used to think I wasn't cut out for it."

Without any basis for thinking so, my parents had decided when I turned twelve that I was fit to care for other people's children. They had volunteered my babysitting services to everyone they knew, and this thankless task had dragged on until I escaped to college.

For five dollars an hour, I'd refereed fights among the older ones and chased them around their houses, struggling to prevent destruction. I'd stopped the little ones from flushing assorted household items and pets down the toilet and tried in vain to cajole them to bed. I'd held the babies at arm's length like ticking bombs and yearned for the return of their parents.

"But," I mused, "I might want kids down the road. I could see that."

The previous fall, I'd been reading at home when my mom stopped by with Molly, a small sparking wire of a five-year-old with a tangle of red curls. Molly was my mom's charge that day, a day that included measuring my windows for curtains.

"I don't need curtains, Mom."

"Everyone needs curtains," she tsked, bustling through the apartment with her tape measure. Over her shoulder to Molly, she said, "I'll just be five minutes. Then we'll go to the park."

Clutching a plush stegosaurus, Molly plopped on the couch

beside me, so close that our legs touched. "Are you my aunt?"

I set my book down. "No. Your dad is my cousin, so that means we're cousins too."

"But you're a grown-up."

"I know. It's a little weird." I paused. "What's your dinosaur's name?"

"Washington."

"Washington?"

"He used to be *president*?"

Her exasperation made me laugh. "Yes. That's right."

She regarded the book on the couch. "I'm in kindergarten. I can read."

"Can you?" I picked up the book, thumbed through it for a manageable sentence, and pointed to it. "What does this say?"

She'd been so pleased with herself after reading it that suddenly we found ourselves playing a game. I located another sentence for her to read, then another, then another, and was disappointed when my mom reappeared, telling Molly to put on her coat. I had liked the feel of the little girl tucked up against me, a little oven generating warmth, her voice small and clear like a bell.

After recalling this story to Dutch, I shrugged. "We'll see."

I told him about my parents, and he told me about his, whose names were John and June.

"John and June," I repeated. I knew *Walk the Line* by heart. "Like Johnny Cash and June Carter. I love that movie. I love their story."

"Meant to be, right?" He nodded. "They loved the name thing too. Everybody did. They got together when they were kids. It seemed like they were supposed to be together."

I started regularly spending the night and kept tripping over the large, unwieldy glass case of superhero figures on the floor beside his bed. It would have made sense proudly displayed in the bedroom of a child, a comic book lover, but it didn't in Dutch's house, which was nicer than most single men's places I'd seen, with hardwood floors and granite counters, a sleek soullessness that he supposed a single man's place should have. All the walls were gray and bare. The leather furniture was excessive. The TV was too big. As I climbed into his bed, I asked about the glass case.

"I trip over it all the time," he told me. "My dad gave it to me."

He said his dad, a vet who had gone to Vietnam and come back a different person, had woken up one morning when Dutch was ten, walked out, and never returned, retreating into silent alcoholic solitude.

I thought then of my own dad, who throughout my childhood had dutifully tacked my artwork to the refrigerator, attended every recital, and now came running to my aid when I got a flat tire. His worst offense, committed unknowingly, was giving me the wrong kind of compliments when I was a teenager.

I also thought, guiltily, that John might have spared Dutch somewhat if he had never been there at all. Maybe leaving behind a pregnant woman or a baby felt easy for some men. Maybe they felt like they were leaving an unformed idea rather than a person. But to abandon a ten-year-old, to know exactly who he was missing and to ensure that the boy did, too, seemed worse. I didn't say that to Dutch.

He almost never heard from his dad after that, Dutch continued. But on his eighteenth birthday, John had surfaced and awkwardly presented him with the case of superheroes, which had been his as a boy, and which Dutch had awkwardly accepted.

"And ever since then, every time I move," Dutch concluded, "I lug it with me." He turned up his hands and let them drop on his stomach. "I don't know what to do with it, so it ends up on the floor."

After John left, June had helped Dutch build his soapbox derby cars. At his scout ceremonies, she had stood alongside all the men presenting badges to their sons and presented Dutch with his. She had sat alone, cheering, in the stands at his baseball games.

I pictured June in a sea of fathers.

"The fucked-up thing is, she still loved my dad after that." Dutch shook his head. "She loves him now. She checks on him, invites him to holidays. He doesn't come, but she invites him. And she stops by his place every couple weeks to bring him money and food and cigarettes."

"She never remarried?"

"Nope. Never even dated anyone. You know, not seriously enough that I ever met him or heard about him. She still wears her engagement ring." Seeing my fascination, he continued. "It's this basic little ring, all he could afford. My grandparents even offered to give him the money for a better one, but he refused, and she's never taken it off. Even though she could buy herself an iceberg if she wanted to." He shrugged. "It's like after my dad, that was it for her."

His mom had sounded unknowable. From old money, a long line of high-profile attorneys, she was the third judge in her family and the first woman, and their family name was a prominent one in their town. This intimate portrait of her moved me.

Some people remained forever walled off from others, I suspected, because their broken places somehow did not correspond. Dutch's brokenness and mine fit together in a way that seemed restorative.

When he talked to me like this, I leaned toward him, nodding. My murmurs came full of empathy, free of judgment. I reached out at different points to touch him. With a transformative power that had always come easily to me, I became a bowl, robin's-egg blue and perfectly smooth, into which others could freely pour.

Sometimes after closing the bar, we returned to his house and sat side by side on his kitchen floor, our intimacy unobstructed by furniture. With our backs against his cabinets, plates of leftovers balanced on our touching legs, we talked with abandon.

Other times we skipped the bar and insulated ourselves in his house for entire weekends, kicked off on Friday evening with a walk to the nearby market for dinner supplies. On one of those Fridays, a heavy, floury snowfall veiled the bare trees and rooftops, and rather than take the streets, we decided to walk along the frozen creek that wound through town, bisecting it. The wooded path was empty and still except for the occasional crunch of our boots on ice or the snap of a branch as we brushed past.

And maybe because of what Dutch had told me about his mom, and maybe because of the snow, a memory came surging to me. I stopped. "Did I ever tell you about my ring?"

Dutch stopped too. "What ring?"

"I had this ring, from my grandmother. I got it when she died. And eight years ago, I walked right through here"—I gestured at the path—"and I lost it. It fell off in the snow."

Growing up, I had shared my cousins' apprehension about going to our grandparents' house. It wasn't about Nan, who always offered a perfumy, slightly brittle hug, but a strain in the air that kept me quiet and well behaved without having to be told. I'd vaguely understood that the source of the strain was my austere grandfather, who, according to family consensus, had never treated Nan very well.

He had appeared only for family meals, saying little, and scaring everyone else into relative silence. Once he had finished eating and left the dining room, oxygen rushed back to it. After shooing my cousins and me out, Nan and her five adult children remained to drink and smoke and play cards.

The backyard had been an acceptable exile, big enough to accommodate our baseball games and makeshift Olympics. But when the weather left no alternative but the basement, a gloomy space devoid of any kind of entertainment, we shuffled down the stairs as if to our execution. Directly above us, we heard the adults having what sounded like great fun.

When we eventually climbed the stairs and swarmed the dining room, armed with grievances and unmet needs and bids for attention, Aunt Peggy and Aunt Maeve shut us down.

"Let the adults talk," Aunt Peggy always said.

"You guys need to figure out ways to entertain *yourselves*," Aunt Maeve snapped, herding our sullen group back downstairs. "You have the whole *basement*."

Our presence, our very existence, had always exasperated my aunts. Describing them to Dutch, I said, "I never understood why people who obviously don't like kids had so many of them."

Sometimes I overheard snatches of conversation between Nan, my mom, my aunts and uncles that sounded heated, bordering on argument. When I heard them say "asshole," I knew they were referring to my grandfather. When I heard them use words like "masochist" and "martyr," I knew they meant Nan, but not what the words meant.

I didn't care. Nan always dressed up, as if perpetually on her way to a party. Her smooth skin betrayed nothing of her decades of smoking. She always wore her trademark burgundy lipstick, and with her dark hair and small waist, I could easily imagine her as young. She was as beautiful and mysterious as a movie star.

I was nine when my mom brought me along on a mission to clean Nan and Grandpa's house. Nan bustled about the kitchen, just back from the mall. She wasn't one to sit on the floor playing with her grandkids and always seemed slightly uneasy with us. But when I peered into her shopping bags, oohing and ahhing at their contents, she'd tilted her head. "Do you like clothes?"

"I like *your* clothes," I said. "Fancy ones."

From then on, whenever my mom cleaned Nan's house, I joined her eagerly. Nan ushered me into her airy, lace-curtained bedroom, an oasis in the tense house. I sat on the flowered bedspread and she went to work in her closet, pulling out old dresses that she piled on the bed, adding armloads of high heels and jewelry boxes.

I loved Nan and her sanctuary, loved dressing up in all of the impossibly glamorous things she spread before me. As I spun and preened for her, she perched on the slipper chair at her vanity table and murmured her approval, sending thin wisps of smoke curling into the air.

When I was twelve, she produced a dainty enameled box that I had never seen before. From it she lifted a ring, which she held out to me. "This one is special. Would you like to try it on?"

I accepted the ring in silent reverence, sliding it onto my finger and extending my arm to admire it: the slim white-gold band, the plump oval sapphire at its center flanked by two small diamonds. Caught in one light, the sapphire looked royal blue, and in another, navy, almost black.

I turned my hand this way and that, repositioning the slightly loose band when the sapphire slipped off center, awestruck by its beauty. And when I breathed, "Nan, I want to be just like you when I grow up," unmistakable surprise and pleasure flashed across her face.

My mom slipped into the bedroom, holding a rag and a can of Pledge. She smiled at us, at the ring. "I haven't seen that one in a while."

To me, Nan said, "You can have that ring someday." To my mom, Nan's voice changed in weight and emphasis, "I want her to have that someday."

Shortly after Nan died, my mom and aunts had withdrawn into Nan's bedroom. I watched my aunts go, noting their matching large, boxy asses and otherwise pointy features: their narrow noses, their cheekbones, their sculpted fingernails. Even their voices formed sharp points, though cigarettes had sanded and blunted Aunt Peggy's.

So began the process of sorting through Nan's possessions, determining what to donate, what to throw away, and what to divide among themselves. I watched as they carried empty boxes in, bulging boxes out. I listened as the bedroom door opened and closed. When the opportunity arose to peek in, Nan's sanctuary was dismantled and stripped bare, her treasures inventoried and dispersed like debris, and Nan seemed to be dying twice.

When the door closed, I hovered outside, listening to my mom and aunts argue. Nan's wedding ring had gone to Aunt Peggy, the oldest. Her pearls had gone to Aunt Maeve, the middle child, and the gold bracelet went to my mom, the youngest. They quickly divvied up the rest of the mostly costume jewelry. But the sapphire ring was a point of contention.

"There's no way that ring is going to a kid," I heard Aunt Peggy say. "It's way too valuable."

"It *is*, Maura." That was Aunt Maeve. "We're her *daughters*. One of us should get it."

I went cold with sorrow. This family shooed kids into the basement. It did not wage war on their behalf.

But just when I thought my aunts had scored a definitive win, when the silence read that way, I heard my mom's voice again, surprising in its authority. "Mom promised her the ring. I'm doing what Mom wanted."

Back at home that evening, my mom had joined me as I sat doing homework at our kitchen table. As she slid the small enameled box across the table to me, something flickered across the grief she had worn for the last month, something different, something new. Victory.

"Take good care of this ring."

For years, I had kept it safe, wearing it out only rarely. But when I was twenty-one, on a night like any other, I decided to wear it to the bar.

I cut through town along the creek. The snow had spread a downy white quilt over the woods. And when I arrived at the bar and squeezed in at my friends' crowded table, I looked down at my cold-reddened hands and realized my ring finger was bare. I had never felt sicker, more panicked.

The ring had always been too big. Why had I never had it sized, or worn it at all on such an ordinary night? When I told my friends, they sprang to their feet and followed me back to the creek, a search and rescue team, slowly walking the path and painstakingly scanning the ground until the darkness forced us to give up.

"I came back here for weeks after that, looking for it," I explained to Dutch. As he stood next to the creek, listening to my story, the snow powdered our hair and jackets and clung to our eyelashes. "I dug and clawed through the snow so many times. And I came back in the spring, thinking maybe I'd find it once the snow melted. But I never did." When his face and body language suggested no impatience, I added, "I almost hope someone found it and wears it and loves it. Seems better than it just being here somewhere buried under dirt and leaves." This thought, this likelihood, made me terribly sad.

I looked wistfully around at the ground, still half expecting to discover the ring glinting at me in the snow. The strength of the memory, the ache of it after eight years, surprised me.

He took my right hand, tugged off my gray knit glove, and kissed my ring finger.

When we fell into bed, we eventually slept, shaped and smoothed into one form within a cocoon of shared blankets and shared breathing, our eyelashes fluttering against each other. He whispered to me about our future.

We, our, us. The language of plurality flowed unhindered. We pried open our vaults.

One person in Dutch's vault was Andy, a friend from his hometown. In high school, Dutch told me, Andy had driven them to a party. They both got blackout drunk, and afterward, Andy dropped Dutch off at home. Before reaching home himself, Andy plowed his car into a tree, sustaining massive internal injuries. Eleven days later, Andy's parents removed him from life support.

"I don't even know why I'm talking about this." Dutch's stories often included this interjection. "I never talk about this."

I pictured the two teenage boys playing baseball, trying to pass some class, trying to get girls. I pictured them side by side in the car, relishing this small taste of freedom, Andy's hands on the wheel, Dutch fiddling with the radio, the incomprehensibility of how radically their fates were about to diverge. "I've never known anyone my age who died."

"It was surreal," Dutch said. "You know, one minute we're driving home, and he was freaking out a little because he thought he was gonna miss his curfew. And then—" He snapped his fingers.

Quietly, carefully, I asked, "How did you hold up when you saw him?"

"I didn't go to the hospital."

I blinked.

"I didn't go to the funeral, either." My shock made him squirm a little. "There's no way I could handle seeing him hooked up to a bunch of tubes, or in a box. I hate hospitals and funerals. I never go."

His revelation thrust me back to my childhood, to a slow, grumbling acceptance of my parents' nonnegotiables. One was church. Another was chores. Another, whenever someone got sick or died, was showing up.

The day before Nan's funeral, I had trailed after my parents into the funeral home, balking in the doorway of the room where she lay, my stomach twisting. When they turned and saw that I had stopped, I said in a small voice, "I don't want to." I had never seen a dead body.

"No one wants to," my mom said.

"It's what you do," my dad said.

They led me up to the casket. Nan's face was all wrong.

Someone had applied heavy, almost stagey makeup and coral lipstick instead of her signature burgundy. As I contemplated the mistake, something else about Nan's mouth struck me. The pursed tightness of her lips made me wonder if they had been somehow fastened on the inside.

My parents lowered themselves to the kneeler. I stood behind them, my eyes on Nan's waxen hands, folded across her chest like a vampire's, rosary beads wound through her manicured fingers.

Sometimes when my parents told me who we were all going

to visit, in a hospital or a nursing home, I had whined, "I don't like those places."

My parents looked at me stonily, and my mom said what I found myself repeating to Dutch. "No one likes those places."

He fidgeted. "It wouldn't have mattered if I'd been there. Andy wasn't even conscious those few days that he hung on. He wouldn't have known."

"His parents would have." Dutch had said they'd been lifelong friends, that growing up, he'd spent almost as much time at Andy's house as his own. "Your mom didn't make you go?"

"She would never. She wouldn't want me to be uncomfortable." He looked uncomfortable now, and I wondered about June. Maybe, in trying to balance the scale weighted against her fatherless son, she had never made Dutch do much of anything.

"But, Dutch…" Again, my parents' exact words resurfaced. I realized as I spoke them how much I really believed them. "It's not about you."

He met my gaze. "You think I'm an asshole."

"*No.* No." I flushed. "You were just a kid. I'm so sorry."

His face showed no anger, no defensiveness or tension. He simply looked at me, listening, wide open to me.

"I just think," I offered in a measured tone, "that sometimes, we need to show up."

When he smiled, the heat of it warmed me. "Going forward, I'll consider making exceptions."

I smiled back. "Like what?"

"Like for my mom. And for you. Down the road. If you still like me."

I already loved him so wholly that I laughed when he said it. And yet, even as I laughed, I heard a finger on a single piano key. Though barely audible, the note sent a shudder through me. *Don't get too comfortable.*

2

We said to each other, "I want to know everything about you." In this we shared an urgency and an effusion, a need to rush at each other all at once.

We asked each other, "Who knows you best?" In this we shared a desire to see all the pieces that others did not.

We said, "I wish we'd always known each other." In this we shared a sense that we had lost something by not finding each other sooner.

Dutch asked me, "What were you like before?"

"Before what? Before you?"

He considered. "What were you like ten years ago?"

Ten years ago. I'd been nineteen. The thought of that period, of myself then, made me shudder. I'd been sick.

I had in fact undergone two illnesses, the first of which relegated me to my parents' couch for a month. I slept, watched TV, and ate little. When I emerged from my stupor, blinking at the light like a newborn, I heard the same compliment again and again. "You look so good."

It shocked me. I had never felt more pallid. But as I studied myself in a full-length mirror, I realized I had, quite by accident, lost some weight. And this affirmation, this tiny triviality, ushered in the second, far graver illness.

In the past, I had wanted a laugh when I called myself "an acquired taste" and bemoaned being eclipsed by my pretty girlfriends. I had been loved by a couple sweet boyfriends, and my looks had never elicited much comment. Once they did, a hunger for that attention sprang to vicious life. I hadn't even known I had it in me.

I also hadn't known that I possessed such a talent for deprivation. I relished my command over the constant gnawing hunger. I cultivated and perfected it.

"What have you been *doing*?" people asked admiringly.

I had always been moderately, unremarkably active. But at nineteen, to press my experiment further, my exercise became incessant and frantic. I learned to batter myself with it, until my collarbone and shoulder blades protruded. People shook their heads. "You look so pretty."

I had longed to be pretty. But I hadn't realized the great deficiency in my appearance until I radically changed it. The more I erased myself, the more visible I became.

I didn't say all this to Dutch—about the illness, about having always been the slightly doughy, entertaining sidekick of prettier girls. I didn't want him to know I had been the kind of person who would make herself so sick, go to such lengths, to garner some petty praise.

I said instead, "I went through a lot of body-image stuff ten years ago. It messed me up. I needed some help with it."

The server set our food down in front of us.

"Help from your parents?"

My laugh confused him. "No, not my parents." I took a bite of my turkey club. "I love my parents, but they didn't really get it."

My transformation had delighted them.

"Everyone at the League wants to know if they can fix you up with their sons," my mom had trilled.

"Yeah, Pat Sheehan was just asking for his boy," my dad said. "You know, he's a fireman," he added approvingly.

"I think the word you're going for is *firefighter*, Dad."

His smile conveyed that he loved me immensely, and that what I'd said was preposterous. "Well, you look great," he boomed. "Whatever you're doing, keep doing it."

I had met their broad smiles with a dull stare.

Much later, grudgingly, I came to terms with their limitations, I told Dutch. "They'd never known anyone with an eating disorder," I explained. "They probably didn't even know what that was, beyond some old Karen Carpenter reference. They weren't"—*what's the right word?*—"equipped."

I had always known they loved me and thought me capable of accomplishing any number of things. I also understood that in their very fabric, what they wanted most for me was a mate, a family of my own. A dramatic weight loss that helped facilitate that process elicited relief, not alarm.

"So what helped you?" Dutch took a bite. "Therapy?"

"Sort of." I had discovered therapy in feminism. It started with Women's Studies and Women's Lit courses in college. "And I know those classes are a joke to a lot of people," I added, remembering male friends' snickering comments at that time. I ran into one in the bookstore with an armload of what he sneeringly called "chick lit." Another consoled a friend who'd been required to take Women's Studies, "Look at it this way, you're gonna be surrounded by girls in there. You'll probably get so much ass."

It occurred to me that this might sound like a joke to Dutch too—that I might. "Know your audience," I always told my students.

So why are you talking to a golfer who watches NASCAR about dead grandmothers, lost heirlooms, anorexia, and feminism? Insecurity swept through me. But when our eyes met, he just looked at me, listening.

I told him I read everything my professors assigned, and then everything I could find. What I read began to make sense of the nonsensical, to order the chaos I felt, to show me that mine was not an isolated, singular submersion. Women like me filled these treacherous waters.

I pored over these writings, lined my shelves with them, consumed them like food, used them like maps. They fed me and gave me a new way of being in the world, in my skin. And the more I understood, the more power I regained.

In other words, I explained to Dutch, I got out of the water.

"How, though?" he asked. "I mean, it's one thing to understand, to believe. It's another to actually *be* different."

"I know. I just wanted to be different. I wanted to get better."

Internally I had experienced a revolution. The external

changes were far more subtle. I continued exercising, moderately. I no longer allowed myself to fixate on my reflection, a compulsion that resembled narcissism but derived from deep self-loathing. I started eating again, moderately, and I did it publicly. Normal people did it all the time.

They never gave it a thought. Or it was an afterthought, like checking the mail. Or it was a task, like getting dressed. Or it was a pleasure to be relished. For me, eating in front of others had caused anguish I had gone to great lengths to avoid, convinced that everyone looked at me and shared the same thought. *She shouldn't be eating that.*

I forced myself to eat in public as part of my self-prescribed recovery. I had practiced, and done it when called to, and I did it then, too, sitting across from Dutch. I took neat, careful bites of my sandwich. It was dinnertime. Normal people did it all the time.

I had not told Dutch every detail. But I had told him far more than I'd ever told a boyfriend before. "I worked hard to be different," I said. "I made some changes. I tried some new things."

"But not therapy."

"I would have gone. I couldn't afford it." No job I'd held as an adult had offered health insurance. "Have you ever been in therapy?"

"Nope. And I never will." His declaration was unequivocal.

"Then you may be part Irish after all." I sipped my water. "And there you have it. Now you know all my secrets."

He chewed thoughtfully.

I wiped my mouth and took another nervous sip. "What do you think?"

He paused. He looked at me. "Body-image stuff and feminism."

"Yeah."

"One as salvation from the other."

"That's fair to say." I felt naked.

"That's…" He searched. "That's not what I thought you would say."

"What did you think I would say?"

"I don't know. I guess something dark."

"The road was pretty dark for a while there." I couldn't keep the defensive edge out of my voice.

"I know. I understand. You just looked so nervous this whole time. I thought you were going to drop something a lot heavier."

"Like what?"

A small smile played at the corners of his mouth. "Like, I don't know, you want me to check out your sex dungeon. That you built behind a secret door in your apartment. Chains and torches and shit." He laughed when he saw my face. "I don't know."

I snickered. "I did build a sex dungeon. I just don't use it anymore."

We relaxed back into each other.

"Does this mean you're really into the Indigo Girls?"

"I love the Indigo Girls," I said earnestly.

He laughed. "How about sturdy sandals? I need to know what I'm working with here."

"I think you're muddling your lesbian and feminist stereotypes. But no, not sturdy sandals." My high heel found his leg under the table. "See?"

He reached down to graze my calf, and a lightness returned to me. "It's your turn. Tell me all your secrets. 'I need to know what I'm working with here.'"

I could account for his smile, but not for the flicker in his eyes. "Okay," he finally said. "I'll tell you all my secrets."

A few nights later at the bar, he asked if I'd ever done any drugs.

"I've smoked weed a handful of times. I didn't like it." I smiled a little through my swig. "I took to the drink just fine, though."

I said it with no self-consciousness. I traveled in a twenty-something Irish Catholic pack that viewed alcohol consumption as a birthright, perfectly respectable and as commonplace in daily life as water. On Saturdays during football season, we arrived at Gaelic Park by noon to drink and watch the games, then hit the bar afterward, for a rough total of fourteen drinking hours.

I spent Sundays recovering with my best friends Claire and Fiona. We holed up in Claire's living room in front of her TV, Claire curled on the loveseat, Fiona and I forming an L on the sectional, with a large bottle of Tylenol and plastic bags of greasy takeout piled on the coffee table between us. Occasionally we sat up to take another handful or bite.

On our last ritual Sunday, I said feebly from my fetal position, "I want you to kill me. I mean it this time."

Fiona shivered and drew a blanket over herself. "I feel bad, you guys." Her hangovers always bloomed into guilt. "Maybe we should take it easy."

Claire dipped her fingers into her glass of water and flicked droplets in Fiona's direction. "I absolve you. Don't feel bad."

And we didn't, not really, never for more than a day. We trusted that this period of harmless excess would pass, that down the road, our families and careers would occupy the forefront of our lives, that alcohol would drift naturally to the side.

Dutch seemed edgy. He told me he'd smoked a lot of weed and still did sometimes. He told me he'd done coke a few times. He told me he'd gone through phases of taking pills.

"What kind of pills?"

"Xanax, Oxy, Vicodin."

This caught me off guard. He hurriedly explained that he didn't take them anymore.

"And what"—I wasn't sure what I wanted to ask—"what was that like?"

"You mean, what did it feel like?"

I considered. "Yeah."

He toyed with a straw. "I guess pills made me not care. No matter what was happening around me, I just didn't care."

"And that was the point? That was how you wanted to feel?"

"I didn't want to feel anything at all. That was the point."

The absence of feeling. "That sounds like death."

He said, almost tenderly, "There's nothing better." Then he broke the brief silence that followed. "Like I said, I'm done with all that. Have been for a long time."

I nodded.

He fidgeted. "Are you judging me? I'm afraid you're judging me."

"I'm not." As he picked his way up this incline, he kept looking over his shoulder to make sure I was still there. "I promise."

He told me that when he was twenty-one, he'd gotten a DUI. He'd gone to jail. He'd lost his license.

"Do you have one now?"

"Nope." He looked down.

I leaned back against the booth, thinking. "You have a car. You drive all the time."

"I know. I'm just careful about it." I felt him waiting for me to speak.

"I know lots of people who've been through that. That was a long time ago. I'm glad you told me."

He looked up. "This doesn't change how you feel?"

His brokenness made me love him more. I was designed to run toward it.

This quality in me grated on Claire. If a drunk stray sidled up to us at a bar, her outright hostility and Fiona's polite chilliness left no room for interpretation. But sometimes the interloper got a shot at me and discovered my willing ear.

At the conclusion of one derailed outing, Claire said sarcastically, "What a fun girls' night. Just you, me, Fiona, and Jeff the Kia salesman."

"I'm sorry." He had talked all night. "Guy's just going through a lot."

"So? You don't know him. You don't owe him a therapy session."

"Claire, his *mom* is sick. And his girlfriend broke up with him. What was I supposed to do?"

Fiona's night had also been ruined, but she was gentler, said nothing. Claire told me flatly, "You're a fly strip for fuckups."

I believed, at my center, in the possibility of redemption.

And I had come to believe, for the first time, that I was beautiful. Dutch made it so. "Look at my girlfriend," he said to no one in particular at a crowded, noisy bar. I wore a pink dress that night, like June Carter's in *Walk the Line*, when she and Johnny Cash first met, backstage. When Dutch looked at me like that, the way Johnny looked at June, every nerve inside me hummed.

In college, my Women's Studies classes had dismantled a belief I hadn't even known I'd held then, that the male gaze determined my value. I imagined my mentors from those courses turning away from me now and throwing up their hands. And still, there I stood in my pink dress, in his warm, generative light, wanting to be nowhere else.

When summer came, he brought me to what he called his cottage. I'd been visiting this lake since childhood, and over the years my memories of these trips had loosely assembled into one: squat, humble house, floorboards perpetually scuffed by sandy bare feet, banging screen door, brightly colored beach towels damp on the deck rail.

Dutch and I pulled up to a gated house perched on a bluff. He unlocked the door and moved deliberately, like a lord, up a long flight of stairs. I followed quickly and quietly, like an intruder.

After the tour I stood on the deck, taking in the sprawl of the house behind me and the sprawl of the lake before me, an expanse of perfect gray glass dotted with freighters. My chest clenched like a fist. And then I felt Dutch behind me, his hands heavy on my shoulders. "I love it here."

And now, he loved me too.

We dropped our duffel bags in the bedroom I liked best, the pretty white one with its own porch swing just beyond the

French doors. Then we collected paper cups, a bottle of cold white wine, a baseball, and gloves and clattered down the steep wooden staircase to the beach.

We spread out on the sand and fell into an easy rhythm. The ball sailed back and forth between us, a brilliant daub of white against the cloudless blue of the sky. Then *slap*—that hard, satisfying contact with old, beat-up leather.

We swam, tore through the woods on mountain bikes to the sand dunes, and sat on the beach, talking with a cooler between us. At night, we ate steaks and drank cold beer on the deck. Then we thundered down the steps, through the blackness, and flung ourselves into the water.

Waking up in the white bed, I wanted to remain under the covers with him, naked and entangled and warm, my hand on his chest as it rose and fell. I wanted to go back to sleep. But a restlessness stirred me. I turned onto my back, then glanced over at the clock. *If I'm fast, I'll be done before he wakes up.*

I extracted myself and showered. I brushed my teeth and arranged my hair in a loose, messy bun. I put on a sundress and examined my reflection. *Don't dwell here.*

Heeding the small, familiar voice with a resolute click of the bathroom light, I spun and slipped barefoot out to the porch swing. Sitting there, I studied the outline of his form in bed and felt a defenselessness that scared me.

At the gentle *creak creak creak* of the porch swing, his eyes fluttered, opened, and drowsily settled on me. When he joined me and draped his right arm around me, his right hand found the thin cotton straps on my shoulder, loosely tied. He toyed with them.

"See that?" His left arm stretched toward the distance, his finger pointing.

I squinted. "What?"

His fingers moved lightly over my shoulder, beneath the straps, sliding them down to my upper arm. "On the lake there. The sandbars."

I saw them then, three long, murky white strips, wavering in the crystalline blues and greens.

"Think you could make it?" A playful challenge.

"I think so. They don't look that far."

He smiled and gave the straps one slow, gentle pull, untying them. "You a strong swimmer?"

"Decent." I shifted my other shoulder a bit. Those straps slid down. "Did you want to swim out there right now?"

"Well. Maybe not *right* now." He eased my dress down further. "But we'll try that sometime."

He pulled me back to the cool, soft white bed.

We howled with laughter through that trip, like when he lit the grill and in one poof, eradicated his left eyebrow and the hair on his left arm, and when the obviously new server at a local restaurant fumbled through the specials, listing one of them as a turd sandwich.

"We'll have that," he told the mortified girl, grinning at her.

Afterward, we settled into deck chairs at the water's edge. He fiddled with the old radio he'd found in the garage and landed on a DJ purring, "104.1, where the lake is for lovers." Dutch didn't change the station. After corny ballads by the Bee Gees, Christopher Cross, and Toto, he didn't change the station.

Finally I turned to him. "This is the stuff retirees play on their pontoon boats."

"If you love me, you have to come with me on this." He leapt out of his chair and snatched me out of mine. "And you have to get in the spirit of things. You heard her. The lake is for lovers." And he tossed me, laughing, into the water.

We spent entire weekends in his living room. During intermission between movies one weekend, we rose from the couch to stretch. He surveyed the comprehensively gray room and said, "I need to do something with this place. What would you do with it?"

I pretended not to feel the weight of the question. "It could use some color," I offered, keeping my voice light. "And books. And plants and art."

I had filled my apartment with these touches to counteract its shabbiness.

He stroked his chin. "Art, like, lace doilies on the furniture? Heart-shaped potpourri dish on the coffee table?"

"No, no." I laughed. "Just some warmth."

"Like your place?"

Suddenly shy, I nodded.

"Your place is warm," he allowed. "It feels like you."

We wore a path between his house and my apartment, always passing a gray clapboard-shingled Cape Cod between them. It sat on a quiet street lined by trees that stretched across the pavement toward each other, as if trying to embrace. Raspberry-hued geraniums stuffed the planter boxes on every window. Dutch and I sometimes paused in front of the house to take in its extraordinary pink garden.

Masses of hydrangeas lined the front of the house, their delicate, dense globes graduating from faint to almost hot pink. Stone tiers held an abundance of cheerful, candy-colored phlox and gerberas. Giant fuchsia hibiscus blooms and roses flanked the stone walk.

"Hell of a gardener," Dutch noted the first time I showed it to him. "Someone loves this place."

"I do," I told him. It looked like a fairytale cottage, where a child might seek refuge.

Then one night, stumbling home from the bar, we came upon the house and saw a FOR SALE sign in the yard.

Dutch stopped in front of it. "I'll buy this for us," he said. "We could live here together. If you'll have me."

He didn't mention it again. He didn't remember. But I did.

3

Dutch and I dated for four years. Early on in our relationship, he shared with me the details of his legal history. He also expressed deep remorse for his actions and for their negative impact on all involved.

What he'd told me was true. At twenty-one, Dutch had been charged with DUI and lost his license. But a week after telling me, he told me the rest of the story, the whole story of that night. He'd partied with his friends. He'd driven home. On the way, he struck someone in the street. In addition to DUI, he'd been charged with a hit and run.

We were lying in bed when he said it. "The girl was fine," he added quickly. "But she did get banged up."

The girl. A girl on foot. I found out more along the way.

Witnesses at the trial included Norma, a woman who lived in the neighborhood where the accident occurred. She testified that she'd been awakened by her whining beagle at one a.m., thrown a coat over her pajamas, and taken the dog out. She testified that she and the dog were walking around the block when she noticed a girl on the sidewalk ahead, walking in her direction. Then she watched the girl cross the grass toward the empty street. As she stepped from the curb, she stumbled.

At that moment, Norma had said on the stand, a car hurtled around the corner, hitting the girl, the impact sending her flying. The car barreled away. Norma said she rushed to the crumpled form on the pavement and made her panicked 911 call.

The cops that came to the scene that night also testified at the trial, Dutch said. Based on Norma's description of the vehicle—dark blue or black, distinct round headlights, box-like outline—they quickly found the damaged Jeep, parked haphazardly in a driveway less than a mile away. Inside the house they found Dutch, passed out face down on his bed. A roommate heard their pounding and let them in.

Dutch had no memory of driving home, he told me, of hitting anything, of waking up surrounded by cops, even of agreeing to go to the hospital with them. They waited during his exam. Once a doctor pronounced Dutch fine, other than a staggering blood alcohol level, the cops took him to jail.

"You don't remember *any* of that?" I didn't know what my face betrayed and felt grateful for the darkness of his bedroom.

"Nope." The way he described it, the entire swath of events had been cut from his mind and removed. Having the story relayed to him over the following days and weeks and months, he said, felt like hearing a story about another person.

"I sat in jail till Monday morning," he told me. June couldn't find a judge who would arraign him and set bail over the weekend. But she had been able to pull other strings, including closed-door meetings with the prosecutor, the police chief, and the arresting officer. She hired Kathleen to represent Dutch.

"Kathleen's hourly rate would blow your mind," he said. "But she was a fucking shark."

June brought him home with her to wait. She paid his way out of his lease. She reinstalled him in his childhood bedroom.

Kathleen told Dutch and June, "Somebody got hurt. There's no way this isn't going to trial."

"And my mom already knew that," Dutch told me. "But you should have seen her face." He stirred beside me. "You have to remember, she was a sitting judge with a fuck-up kid. So even though the trial was moved to a different city, we knew it would be all over the news. We knew it would be a big story. Everyone would know what happened. Everyone would be watching."

In my mind then I saw June, palely facing the prospect of her son's trial. Like any parent, she would have agonized over his unknown fate. She would have steeled herself for the humiliation of the entire spectacle. *Everyone would be watching.*

Dutch told me that the community had admired the wealthy and successful Van Lokerens for generations. Surely then, some people also envied them. Surely some would have savored the idea of the crown prince standing trial. I pictured June staring down this likelihood. Some would have watched her son's life shatter like glass and enjoyed it.

In the dark I asked Dutch, "How did your mom hold up?"

"Like a champ, in front of people. Especially at the trial. She never flinched." I pictured June sitting behind Dutch in the courtroom. "But at home, we fought like dogs. She was a wreck."

I knew, from what Dutch had told me, how hard June had tried to give him every possible opportunity. I knew she had tried to give him the map that a father was supposed to provide. But she had been called to collect him from his brand-name prep school every time he got suspended for fighting. She had found weed in his sock drawer and, later, a bottle of Vicodin in his gym bag. She had, late one night, answered a knock at the door in her bathrobe and found Dutch on the porch with a cop, who'd caught him and the police chief's son drinking in a parking lot.

Maybe the cop had already known who the boys were. Maybe they had told him. Either way, taking them home, instead of to jail, showed prudence.

When the cop told June he might not be able to help next time, June told him there wouldn't be a next time. "But with me," Dutch said, "there was always a next time."

After each incident, June thundered away at him, doling out tough love, threats, ultimatums. How, I wondered as I listened to him, did a parent bear a child's missing or broken pieces? Perhaps she had confided in someone who would keep her secrets and reassure her that Dutch's youthful blunders would soon be outgrown and forgotten. Perhaps June had nodded along, agreeing, wanting to agree. Perhaps the voice inside her had whispered something else. *You don't understand. My boy is different.*

"You have to remember, too," Dutch said, "she watched me get out of Andy's car right before he crashed it. She got the call from Andy's dad. She went to the hospital and sat with his parents. And she went to the funeral. She was there for all of that." When I heard the wobble in his voice, I wondered if he appreciated the darkness of the room too. "So when all this shit happened with me and my trial, Andy had only been gone for four years. It was still *really* fresh in her mind. That didn't help."

So while June hadn't made Dutch go to the hospital or the funeral, she had been there the whole time. I pictured her in a hospital, sitting beside a motionless and broken teenage boy as machines beeped. I pictured her in a church, her gaze on the incomprehensible casket.

And then, only four years later, another drunk-driving accident. Another teenager, not killed at least but nearly, lying in a hospital. And this time, her son behind the wheel, so close to tragedy, almost beckoning it. It must have seemed like death was written on him.

Lying beside Dutch, I thought suddenly of a playground song from childhood: *First comes love, then comes marriage. Then comes baby in a baby carriage.* The chanty, singsong tune in my head remained the same, but the words changed: *First he's the passenger, then he's the driver. Then—*

I stopped myself.

Dutch told me the things June screamed at him as they circled each other in the house. "'Your friend *died* this way. What more do you need to learn this lesson? You could have killed that girl. What's the *matter* with you?' She was scared," he went on. "I was too. But I couldn't do anything. You can't unring a bell. All we could do was wait for the trial."

He'd been stunned when the court scheduled the trial to begin right before Christmas. He remembered exploding, "Three *months*? Why does it take that long?"

He remembered June saying, "That's actually very fast. You're lucky."

He said he watched TV and went nowhere except to his random drug and alcohol tests. He said they paced the house. He said they waited.

As he talked, my eyes adjusted to the darkness.

Kathleen had been confident about the failure-to-stop charge but warned of the likelihood of a DUI conviction. "People *hate* drunk drivers. They're pariahs nowadays. That's just the culture."

To me, Dutch added, "*Pariah.* I never forgot that word." He got up to use the bathroom and returned. "That's how I felt, though, sitting through the trial and listening to—all of that." He tripped over the case of superheroes, climbed back into bed, and resumed. "I felt like a fucking monster. Do you know what it's like to sit in a roomful of people who hate you?"

The closest I had come was when I returned a batch of dismal grades to a group of scowling, entitled college students. "No." My voice matched the quiet of the room.

In her opening statement, Kathleen told the jury that on the night in question Dutch had attended a party. She told them he drove home when he shouldn't have, and that his car struck a pedestrian. She told them that these were the undisputed facts of the case.

At this declaration from his own attorney, Dutch said he'd glanced back at the girl's parents, sitting in the gallery. "They looked so triumphant."

But what the jury didn't know, Kathleen continued, were the circumstances that led to the accident. "Because that's what this was. An unfortunate accident."

Did it matter? Dutch had hit this girl. Kathleen had said so herself. But with culpability in question, she argued, intent mattered a great deal.

Dutch said that he didn't look at the girl's parents again. Except for the occasional echoing cough, they sat in obedient silence throughout the trial.

He didn't know that he had struck a person, Kathleen maintained. That explained why he didn't stop and call the police, why he drove home, why he left his Jeep in the driveway, in plain sight, and went to bed. If he had known what had happened and wanted to conceal it, he would have hidden himself and the visibly damaged car.

A variety of factors had contributed to the accident, Kathleen argued, factors that would have put a completely sober driver in the exact same situation. One was that it was nighttime, which created a visibility issue. And even the most experienced drivers had at some time or another inadvertently struck an object at night. A garbage can that had rolled into the street, an animal, a pothole.

Another factor, perhaps the most critical, was timing. Precisely when Dutch had turned onto this particular street, the girl stumbled right into it.

Kathleen eviscerated the stammering girl during cross examination. "You recall walking on the sidewalk."

"Y-yes."

"You recall moving toward the street."

"Um...yes."

"Did you intend to cross the street?"

No, that had not been the girl's intention. When Kathleen asked her why she had moved into a street she had not intended to cross, the girl said the reason was her shoes.

"Her shoes?" I interrupted.

"Yeah, she said she was wearing really high heels that night, and they'd been killing her feet for hours."

I thought tenderly then of the girl, cursing her hateful heels. They always seemed like a good idea at the beginning of the night.

"She said she thought about taking them off and walking barefoot but decided to walk in the street instead. She said it looked smoother than the sidewalk."

But the girl, Kathleen repeatedly pointed out, had attended a party, like Dutch. She had been drinking, like Dutch. Her blood alcohol level had been tested at the hospital, like Dutch. The only difference between them was that the girl was underage.

"Is it possible that your"—Kathleen paused—"*intoxication* contributed to your decisions that night?"

Dutch told me that he and Kathleen had discussed the risk beforehand. She'd said, "If I'm too aggressive, I'll lose the jury.

I'll come across like I'm picking on the victim." But the girl fell victim to her own choices, Kathleen stressed in court, not Dutch's. He could not possibly have anticipated her sudden presence in the street. No one could have.

I turned in bed to face him. "So she was coming home from a party."

"A frat party, she said."

"And she was alone."

"She went there with her roommates, I guess. But she walked home alone."

They let her walk home alone. In college, my own girlfriends and I had followed a strict policy prohibiting abandonment. But maybe this girl's friends had paired off and forgotten her. Maybe the threads of these friendships were more loosely woven than the girl had realized.

I wrapped my arms around my pillow. "What was it like seeing her?"

Dutch shuddered. "Kathleen said to look directly at her when she spoke because I'd seem uncaring and guilty if I didn't." He told me that she only entered the courtroom when called to testify, and that as she hobbled toward the stand on her crutches, they made rubbery, faintly metallic *thunk thunk* sounds against the floor. He told me he looked down.

In doing so, he said, he got a good look at the bottom half of her. "She was wearing a long dress, but I saw a tattoo down by her ankle. A heart. Or I think it was supposed to be a heart. It looked kind of botched."

Just the sort of tattoo I imagined an eighteen-year-old girl getting. She probably couldn't afford a decent artist.

Once the girl was seated on the stand, her crutches leaned against the wall behind her, Dutch had forced himself to look up. When she started speaking, her voice excruciatingly soft and wobbly, he couldn't bear to listen.

"Torn ACL… I had surgery… Concussion… Rib fractures…"

He said he tried to focus on her face. Though only slightly

younger than he was, she looked like a kid.

"Constant pain… Still get dizzy, headaches, can't sleep… Nothing can be done for broken ribs, they hurt every time I take a breath…"

He said she was blond, cute.

"I'm still in physical therapy for my knee…had just started school and had to take the semester off to recover…had to quit my job and move home…"

He said she looked like countless other girls he'd seen at parties. When she finished her testimony and exited the courtroom, her parents stood and followed her.

In her closing argument, Kathleen told the jury that it would be easy, convenient, tempting, to make a snap decision. A driver had struck and injured a young woman because he was drunk. Her injuries were indeed unfortunate. But the truth of the case, if they set emotion aside and carefully weighed the facts as the law required them to, was this: the young woman's impairment, not Dutch's, had caused the accident. It contributed to her poor judgment and poor balance and, ultimately, her injuries. Kathleen just hoped that the jury never found themselves behind the wheel in such a terrible, unforeseeable situation.

Dutch said he liked Kathleen's contrast with the assistant prosecutor, who in his estimation depended too much on maudlin appeals. He liked that Kathleen didn't particularly need the jury to like her or him. She only needed them to see the picture as she had painted it.

On the charge of failure to stop and identify after personal injury, they returned a not guilty verdict just two hours after closing arguments. On the DUI, he got two years' probation and his license revoked.

"That's *it*?" He told me he heard the girl's parents sputtering as he hurried past them in the hallway afterward. "I'm sure they thought their case was a slam dunk. But, you know, they underestimated Kathleen. And they probably didn't understand the weight our name carried." I winced. "I hate to say it, but it's true."

Kathleen told him afterward not to worry about probation. She said she could get him out of it if he kept his head down for a year.

"So that's what I did." Dutch laced his fingers behind his head and stared up at the ceiling as he talked. "I stayed out of the bar, went to AA meetings twice a week, asked someone to sign my attendance slip before I left. I went in for testing whenever they called me but it wasn't like before the trial. Kathleen had this guy in her pocket, and he never actually tested me for anything, just made me fill out questionnaires. And I got a bunch of people to write bullshit letters saying I was sober."

I also wrote letters for him, to him. The inception of our relationship had brought me to the practice.

We never separated for more than a day or two. But when he moved out of range even briefly, I wrote real letters by hand and mailed them, because an email or a text would never do. I constructed them like monuments, using red envelopes and my Waterman pen, a perfect weight in my hand, its rushing black ink tattooing my heavy, creamy stationery like sacred scrolls. These were letters from another era, the kind no one received anymore. But if they did, they would know, without even opening them, the significance of their contents, would gently bundle them together, tuck them away, save them.

Sometimes I filled pages. Sometimes I wrote simply, *Please, when you get this, come over.*

I couldn't imagine writing the type of letters he was describing, these collections of brief, businesslike lies. Our eyes met again, but I lowered mine.

"Then a year later, Kathleen filed a motion for my probation to be terminated. And it was. That was it."

"That was it? Can anyone do that?"

"No. You can't have a prior record, and you have to stay out of trouble during probation, obviously. You need all the documentation I had, plus you have to pay all your fines and pay for a decent lawyer. It cost my mom a fortune."

I thought then of the students who brought me attendance

verification forms to fill out for their probation officers. Some of them, hovering uneasily over me as I completed the forms, told me their circumstances. Maybe they thought they had to. They were on probation for weed, mostly, or for some minor theft.

They were always boys, always Black and brown. Many of these same students fretted privately to me about the laptops and textbooks they couldn't afford, the problem of getting to and from campus on the notoriously unreliable city bus. Through the winter they arrived late to class, sodden and shivering. I'd always wondered how long they remained shackled to the legal system for some petty offense from their teens.

I understood the fragility of Dutch's disclosure, of my response to it. But I couldn't stop myself.

"You do realize that if you were Black, or poor, or both, you'd *still* be sitting in jail."

"I absolutely do." Hearing his certitude, I took a breath. "Trust me, I know the deal. I saw it. I met so many people in AA who were just fucked. They were already barely getting by when they got the DUI, then they got all these fines they couldn't pay that just kept piling up, and then a lot of them lost their jobs because they couldn't get to them anymore, without a license." He looked at me. "Court's a racket. It's like this machine, and once you get stuck in it, there's no way out." He paused. "Unless, you know."

I knew. I had never imagined myself on this side of such a conversation.

He'd heard that getting a license reinstated was much more difficult, if not impossible. He said he might try one day. "But all I wanted to do when this whole nightmare ended—once the dust had settled and I had finished probation—was move. I just wanted to get out of there and start over. So I moved a few times and ended up here."

"What did your mom say about you moving?"

He smiled wanly. "She didn't protest too much."

I pushed my hair out of my face, thinking. "What happened

to the girl?"

"I told you, nothing." For the first time, his tone cut me. "She was lucky."

I wondered how many times she had heard that from family and friends, from doctors and physical therapists. I imagined her lying on her parents' couch, her body broken, her new freedom hardly tasted before being snatched away. She probably hadn't felt very lucky.

"My life got pretty messed up, though," Dutch said. "If you get a DUI in this state, you can't ever get it expunged. It follows you forever."

I lay there, stinging and groping for words to draw him back. "It sounds like your mom was a rock."

"Yeah." He softened. "I never heard a peep from my dad, even though he knew the deal. No phone call, no 'how ya holdin' up.' Nothing. But she had my back. No matter how bad it got, she was right there."

Ominous clouds had momentarily blotted out the sun. With full, dazzling force, it reemerged when he reached for me.

I couldn't process his story with him, beside him, at his house. I went home the next day.

That Sunday, I surveyed the glum evidence of my weekend-long absence: dirty dishes in the kitchen sink, dirty laundry heaped in a basket, an unfinished lesson plan for the following Monday. I felt too unsettled for chores. I almost pulled out my phone to call Dutch.

I had pounced on him for his privilege. It was so glaring and gross. But—I felt a small stab of conscience—he had not done the same to me when I'd revealed my own.

I roamed my apartment, thinking about it. Without question, privilege had allowed him to step out of the legal system unscathed. But it had also allowed me to indulge my eating disorder, and that was what it had been: an indulgence, albeit born of self-hatred. It was an oddly luxurious illness, not striking arbitrarily like so many others, but reserved for those who could afford utter self-involvement, for those with access to food so secure, so unfailingly, unquestionably abundant, that they had the freedom to refuse it.

What would people without this basic necessity have said about my illness? In the throes of it, I had sometimes wondered. It might have seemed comical, if not such an outrage. What would hungry, desperate people have done, ten years earlier, if they had seen me push away the full plates set in front of me? The thought had made me radiate with shame then, and it still did. I considered an eating disorder the quintessential white-girl illness.

I sat down on my couch, stood, and sat back down. Then I resumed my aimless wandering. I'd always considered myself squarely working middle class. But Dutch's story reminded me again of our commonality. *Oh. It's you.*

And the story itself—I replayed it as I wandered. It had all happened years earlier. It was over.

Why didn't it feel over?

Maybe, I speculated, because it haunted him. I'd seen it. But there was something else. *What about the girl?* I sat down again, picturing her walking home through the neighborhood.

It would have been quiet that late at night, except maybe for distant, receding music and the hoots of partygoers. It would have been very dark. How had she felt, teetering through the darkness, when headlights suddenly thrust her into the violent glare? Had she remembered afterward the sensation of flying, weightless, before being plunged into black silence?

I thought again of the chores waiting for me. I eyed my closed laptop and clicked my fingernails on it, vacillating. Finally I opened it and googled Dutch, furtively, as if he might pop up at any moment over my shoulder.

As I scrolled, I realized that he had somewhat undersold the prominence of the Van Lokerens. An avalanche of articles about the family came at me, page after page, at least twenty of them about his trial. The local media had covered it exhaustively.

I scrolled and scrolled, finding no substantive information that Dutch hadn't already told me, and almost none at all about the girl. One article mentioned that she'd been a college freshman, a nursing major. It said that she and four other girls, also freshmen, had shared a two-bedroom rental on campus. I wondered when I read that whether cramming into that house together, living away from their parents, had been these girls' first real adventure.

The picture accompanying the article told me much more. It showed four of the five roommates on the night of the accident, before they left for the frat party. Presumably the missing fifth roommate had taken the picture and submitted it to the newspaper.

The four girls in the picture had crushed together, arms around one another's shoulders and waists. With their giant grins, they looked impossibly young and optimistic, and three of the four wore jeans and T-shirts. The girl from the accident, though, wore a tissuey pink dress and the towering heels debated at the trial. This snapshot endeared her to me even more.

Her friends' choice of jeans and T-shirts had not deterred her. Maybe she hadn't realized that almost everyone at a frat party would be wearing this sloppy uniform. Maybe she hadn't cared. A girl who dressed up for a frat party, I mused, would have envisioned meeting someone special.

But she'd walked home alone. My own experience made me suspect that the party had proven a vast disappointment, spent clutching a Solo cup full of mostly foam and shooing away guys who stumbled and slurred.

In the picture, the girl laughingly clutched her friend as if to steady herself, and when I looked closer, I noticed that they wore matching necklaces. Two small gold crosses on two dainty gold chains. As a teenager I'd had friendships like this, too, where one was as essential to the other as oxygen, requiring constant consultation and communication throughout each day.

And there—I squinted a little—the tattoo Dutch had glimpsed in court, carelessly placed, not quite on her ankle or her lower calf but seemingly floating between them, unanchored. The heart looked slightly lopsided, and the black outline wobbled, thicker in some places than others.

A girl with a cross on her necklace. Maybe getting the tattoo had allowed her an uncharacteristic rebellion.

Two other photos caught my attention. One was of Dutch in the courtroom, and this glimpse of him at twenty-one shook me. Though taken only eight years earlier, the Dutch in the picture was not the man I knew. Despite the immaculately tailored suit and polished oxfords, I saw a boy, his young face arranged into an impassive mask.

I felt another stab, guilt this time. This search was a betrayal. *What are you looking for?*

The last photo showed June, also in the courtroom. I leaned in closer to search for clues but found an image of flawless composure. Her body language and expression divulged nothing. She looked only to be listening intently, as if unaware of the hot, bright spotlight trained on her.

Looking at this picture, I wanted to know her. I wondered if I ever would. Then, a couple months later, she announced to Dutch that she was coming to town.

4

She usually stays in a hotel when she visits," Dutch told me. "But she says she's staying with me this time." In preparation, he scrubbed and purged his house of empty bottles and cans while I dusted and washed dishes.

I sank into the couch, assessing our work. He jogged upstairs. When he returned, he sat down next to me and handed me a small square box, smiling and silent in response to my wide-eyed shock. In the second I took prying open the box, tasting and feeling my whole heart in my mouth, I thought he was proposing.

In the box, a sapphire ring. Nan's beautiful sapphire ring. My head snapped toward Dutch, and the first stupid, incredulous words that came to mind tumbled out. "You found it."

He laughed. "No. I didn't."

Transfixed, I lifted it from the box and slid it on. Its coolness encircled the warmth of my finger, and I became aware not of a conscious decision, but of something already decided. I would never, ever take it off.

He leaned toward me. "Does it look the same?"

"It looks exactly the same." I gaped at it, then at him, then at the ring again. The only difference between it and Nan's was that this one fit perfectly. "How did you do this?"

"You told me the story. You told me what it looked like. Remember?"

I'd forgotten.

"I know I can't replace your grandmother's ring. But you were so sad about it. It seemed so important." His words came in a self-conscious rush. "I went to a couple stores and looked around online, but I couldn't find exactly what you described. I just wasn't sure. So I had it made." He leaned forward again. "Are you sure it's right?"

"It's perfect." I slowly shook my head. "It's the nicest thing anyone's ever done for me."

His face flushed and broke into a wide, satisfied grin. Slowly I removed my clothes. Slowly I climbed onto him, snaked my arms around his neck, and entwined my fingers, adjusting to the ring's new presence there. When I slid him inside me, we breathed, not moving, until the stillness became unbearable.

The next morning, we slept in late. He stretched and hunted through the tangle of sheets for his boxers. "My mom and I are going out to dinner when she gets in tomorrow. Do you want to come?"

June loomed in my imagination. I understood that Dutch needed to live two hours away from her, away from her watchful eye, but also that I couldn't fully know him without knowing her too. She was and had always been absolutely central to him.

I had wondered if this invitation would come. He'd told me he liked distinct bifurcations and that in the past, he hadn't brought girlfriends around his friends. He hadn't accompanied them to their family functions, and he hadn't included them in his. "Too messy," he'd said.

He hadn't wanted his family and friends in the same shared space, and when his mom came to town, he hadn't introduced her to anyone. Until now.

When I joined Fiona and Claire that night and showed them my ring, Fiona exclaimed, "He wants to *marry* you!"

I laughed. "I don't know about that."

"What do you mean, you don't know?" Jubilant, she took my hand and angled the ring toward me as evidence. "You know."

"He says he doesn't ever want to get married. Or have kids."

This news bewildered Fiona. "Why not?"

"He just doesn't, I guess because of his own family." I tried for nonchalance, as I had when Dutch first told me. "He said it from the beginning."

"But that was in the beginning," she insisted. "People change their minds."

Claire cautioned me, "I wouldn't get on this train if I were you."

Fiona thrusted my hand toward Claire. "Men don't give women rings unless it means something."

To me, Claire said, "It means something." To Fiona, she said, "If he's telling her who he is, and who he isn't, she should believe him."

Fiona waved her off. "People change their minds all the time. Especially when they meet the right person."

Contemplating the ring, I thought of what Dutch had said in front of the house with the pink garden. *We could live here together. If you'll have me.* "Maybe. I didn't think I'd meet his mom, and that's happening tomorrow night."

"Amazing!" Triumphant, Fiona turned to Claire, who put her hands up.

"Okay, okay. Calm down." She polished off her beer. "When's he going to meet your parents?"

"He did," I said, and I told them the story.

The meeting had happened by chance. Dutch and I had gone to the bar, not realizing my parents were meeting a large group of friends there for dinner. When they'd spotted us and made their way over, the introductions and pleasantries that followed couldn't have gone more smoothly.

I didn't tell Claire and Fiona about the Saturday after the impromptu meeting, when I had picked Dutch up for a ballgame and turned into my parents' neighborhood on the way. "Quick pit stop."

When I pulled into their driveway, he clutched the passenger armrest, alarmed. "This is your parents' house?"

"Yeah, I'm dropping this off." I'd gestured at the dilapidated box overtaking my back seat, bulging with my old books and chipped dishes, a contribution to my parents' upcoming garage sale.

Dutch squirmed beside me. "Are they here?"

"Well, they live here." I opened the car door. "Will you give me a hand with this thing?"

His hand hovered at the door handle. "I can't. I'm not up for it."

"It weighs a ton." My back still burned from lugging the box to my car. "This will just take a minute."

"I can't. You got this though, right?" He'd been almost pleading. "You got this."

Noting my parents framed in their large picture window, I grimly seized the hulking box.

As I staggered toward the house with it, my dad moved as if to help me. I shook my head to stop him and proceeded into the kitchen, dropping the box with a groan. My parents rounded the corner.

"Garage sale stuff," I'd panted.

They looked at the box. They looked at me. My dad asked, "Is that Dutch out there?"

"Yeah, and we gotta go." I tried to take a normal breath. "We're going to a game."

I felt my parents watching through the window as I left and didn't look back. I didn't want to see their faces.

"I can't believe we actually met him last week," Claire said. "I was starting to think you made him up."

Dutch and I had been dating for months by then. In that time, he had twice agreed to meet my friends and twice texted me to cancel at the last minute.

I had sailed smiling through both nights, pretending his absence didn't matter. Fiona and Claire had been tactful enough to do the same. And maybe it didn't matter, I reasoned afterward. Maybe, like Dutch, I didn't need to merge every part of my life. Maybe I needed to relinquish the childish notion that my friends and I formed one unit.

But then our friend James threw a birthday party at Ginty's, his uncle's pub where he tended bar. All of our friends were going, and Dutch had accepted my invitation. I'd waited and waited for him to back out.

As we drove to Ginty's together, he practically fluttered with nerves beside me.

"My friends are completely down to earth," I reassured him. "Please, don't worry."

And that night, as I'd watched him chatting with Fiona and Claire, watched James throw an arm over his shoulders as they took a shot together, watched the entire group fold him in as if he'd always been there, I'd shone, unable to stop smiling. He'd made an exception, and he was making another one by bringing June and me together. I felt the plates beneath our relationship shifting.

"Now you know he's a real person," I told Claire. "He was happy to meet you guys."

"We were happy to meet him," Fiona said, admiring my ring. "Dutch is great."

She had news too. A series of recent dates with Denny, a new teacher at the elementary school where she taught, seemed to be flourishing into a full-blown relationship.

I tempered my desire to talk at length, to analyze and speculate and dwell. I sensed Fiona holding back as well. We didn't want to be the kind of women who were only capable of talking to other women about men. We also felt we owed a measure of restraint and sensitivity to Claire, who was single. She was always single.

Claire almost never reported any interesting prospects, even when asked, and sometimes we prodded. "Claire, you're an engineer. You're surrounded by men every day. You wouldn't give *any* of them a shot?"

"They won't give me one," she replied. "Men don't like me because I don't need anything from them."

No, no, no, Fiona and I protested. That wasn't true.

"It *is* true," Claire said. "I have a good job, my own house, my own money. I don't need anything. And most men find that unattractive."

We murmured our dissent.

"I'm not going to pretend to be an incompetent, either," Claire continued. "Like, I'm not going to let a guy walk ahead of me and put his name in at the restaurant and order the wine, all that stupid shit, just so he can feel like a man. I'm not." She shrugged. "Also unattractive. Two strikes."

Noble Claire. She would not soften the shape of herself, would not blunt any of her edges and angles, to make herself more pleasing. And still, Claire was alone—Claire, who I knew wanted love, who said so in her matter-of-fact way.

Aloud I said to Claire, "The right person will appreciate a woman who has her shit together." *But maybe you could learn to bend a little.*

My silent admonishment betrayed us both. It reminded me of what Dutch had said when I first told him about finding feminism. It was one thing to understand, to believe. It was another to actually *be* different.

Maybe, despite my efforts to actually be different, I was still bending enough for Claire and me both. Maybe our malleability and our appeal went hand in hand. Maybe we could be loved or we could be principled, but we could not be both.

"What should I call your mom? 'Your Honor'?" I paced Dutch's floor while we waited for June to arrive. "I hope this dress is okay. I mean, I want to look nice, like I'm making an effort, but not trying *too* hard, you know?" I went to the bathroom several times.

As I stood in front of the mirror, again smoothing my dress and hair, again checking my reflection, I heard the familiar voice. *Don't dwell here.* And then I couldn't, because then, June arrived.

When she walked into the house she had bought Dutch, and hugged him, I took in the surgical slice of her bob, the rustle of her cashmere, the faint trail of lilac perfume. Then she turned to me and shook my hand. After introductions, she looked skeptically around Dutch's living room. "It isn't always this clean, is it?"

The question seemed directed at me. "He may have had a little help with this one."

June smiled. We went to dinner.

Throughout the blur of the meal, I tried to make a good impression while simultaneously absorbing every detail of their interaction. This peek into a previously obscured part of Dutch and his life enthralled me.

June was alternately authoritative and easygoing, full of questions and directives, quick to roll her eyes and laugh. Dutch was accommodating and deferential, mildly exasperated by her interrogations, skilled at fending them off with good-natured protests and jokes.

I liked June. I could imagine her in flowing robes, defendants quaking before her, but she was accessible to me, showing a softness in Dutch's presence that maybe she didn't or couldn't in other settings. We all talked easily.

Before the food arrived, June reached across the table and took my hand, her eyes on my ring. "Very nice." Then she turned to Dutch, still smiling. "Very nice."

So she knew. She had known.

For just that moment, as our hands touched, so did the backs of our rings, my sapphire and June's ring from John, the one Dutch had told me about: a thread of a gold band, plain except for a tiny diamond, the modest fruits of a teenager's labor. Seeing it, I felt a kinship, an unspoken recognition.

She was studying me, too, and I felt her leaning toward me as the dinner progressed. I was warm without being overly familiar and well-mannered without affect. I landed a couple tasteful jokes.

Did she see how my love radiated, how happy Dutch looked? Probably. But I knew she took note when I switched to water after nursing one glass of wine, and when I went home after dinner instead of back to Dutch's house with them. June would notice two toothbrushes in the cup on the bathroom counter, but she would still appreciate my graceful departure.

Saying our goodbyes, June pulled me into a sturdy hug. I practically skipped home, sensing that some heavily fortified gate had swung open.

When she left two days later, Dutch summoned me to his

house with an urgency that scared me.

"What's wrong? What happened?"

"Just come over."

When I rushed in a couple minutes later, I found him sitting on his couch, dazed and clutching a folded slip of paper, which he handed me. "My mom gave me this."

I opened it. It was a million-dollar check.

The money, and there would be more to come, June had told him, had always been there, waiting. She had wanted the right moment. But in the midst and aftermath of his legal woes, she said, his fate was too uncertain. She said she had waited for him to graduate from college, which he never did. She said she had waited for him to start a family, which he declared he never would.

"Now," she had told him when she gave him the check, "you need to start making a life for yourself. Start a business, invest, do what you want. But do something. It's time."

Once he had explained it all, we stood side by side, each holding a corner of the check, gazing at it in wonder.

The money became a running joke between us.

"Let's both get tons of plastic surgery."

"Let's start an orphanage where we make the kids change the channels for us all day."

"We should get some exotic pets. How much are giraffes?"

We. The language of plurality flowed unhindered. But despite our endless jokes and conversations about it, no "we" existed where the money was concerned. Did it draw him from me? Did it open a gulf between us? I secretly wondered and worried. Now he could pass through doors that for me remained closed.

Shortly after Dutch received the money, we ran into Glick, who told us about his new girlfriend. Glick lived in the throes of new, consuming, short-lived infatuations, so Dutch and I placed a friendly wager. I said the new girlfriend would last at least three months. Dutch said less than one.

He won the bet and held me to it, and I paid for dinner at a restaurant of his choice. As we sat eating filet, he crowed over his victory, and I tried to mimic his lightheartedness. As I slid my debit card into the server's book, draining the last $150 from my checking account, anxiety ricocheted through me.

He needed my presence, as I did his. I still wanted him inside me or at least near, touching me, all the time.

Still, again, I heard that depression of a single piano key and was unnerved by the note. *Don't get too comfortable.*

I touched and turned my ring and tried to shake away the recurring theme in all the stories Dutch had told me. He had never secured himself to anyone for very long.

I remained in his sunlight. He poured himself into the smooth, robin's-egg blue bowl of me. But I felt a rising, a threat of overflow that perhaps the bowl could not hold. The bowl had always been enough before. The possibility that it couldn't be with Dutch, with whom it mattered most, scared me.

As we sat at Hurley's one night, talking with the other regulars and watching a baseball game on TV, Glick walked in with a man he immediately, proudly introduced. "This is my dad." The man wore glasses but was otherwise Glick exactly, an uncanny preview of what our friend would look like in his fifties.

They took the last two free stools at the bar and ordered the same kind of beer. They made small talk with Dutch and me and the others. They paused mid-sentence to yell at the TV, like everyone else. Our group immediately and seamlessly absorbed them.

Dubious, Dutch eyed the drink Clever had made for him. "That's pretty pink."

"I call this one Jail Bait," Clever announced.

"That's a cosmo, man," Kevin interjected.

"That's a chick drink," Glick declared.

Dutch told Clever, "Lose the lime."

Clever plucked the garnish from the rim.

"I'm gonna need a different glass."

Clever transferred the drink from a martini glass into a squat, stemless one.

"And more booze."

Clever added more vodka and clicked the glass down on the bar in front of Dutch. "Jail Bait."

I chatted and drank my beer, more adept, since meeting Dutch, at being the only woman in a group of men. I knew when to be demure and when to be one of the boys, when to flash a smile or my intelligence like a badge, when to talk and when to remain quiet during sporting events, when to fire a joke like a single shot.

Glick and his dad reminded me of me and my dad, the way they joked together, their ease in each other's company. Each time they finished a beer, Glick's dad gave the same cheerful response to his son's goading. "One more round. But don't tell your mother. I don't want to get in trouble."

Sitting beside me, Dutch swirled and sipped his pink drink. I felt a shift in him, a clouding over I didn't understand and couldn't stop.

We all wound down the night together, staying till last call and leaving as a group. As we called goodbyes across the parking lot, Glick's dad added, "Thanks for letting his old man tag along!"

They went one direction, boisterous. Dutch and I went another, subdued.

"Everything okay?" I ventured as we staggered back to his house.

Yes, just drunk, he said. Just tired. We climbed the stairs to his bedroom, as we had done many times. He tripped over the case of superheroes by his bed, as he had done many times. And this time, his eyes narrowed on it and surged with an all-encompassing rage.

"Piece of shit." Before I knew what was happening, he stomped the case, its glass doors blooming a web of glittering fractures, almost beautiful. "Fuck you. Fuckin' hate you. Fuckin' piece of shit." He stomped again and again with a force that stunned me, the crunch of splintering wood, the chimes of breaking glass. Shards sprayed the floor like bits of ice.

Finally, Dutch snatched the trampled shell of the case and hurled it across the room, where it tore a ragged hole in the drywall and dropped to the floor. He dropped into bed. And all the while I stood in the doorway, watching, breathless.

5

D*utch told me that he had been committed to his sobriety since the time of the accident. Drugs and alcohol were not part of our interactions, and at no point did I observe him using either.*

We drank together constantly.

Sometimes we still charged into the bar like sidekicks and superheroes, Johnny Cash and June Carter belting "Jackson" into one microphone, making each other and the people around us laugh, leaving hand in hand. I drank more with him than I ever had before. I wanted to go where he went.

My church was his house, where we still enclosed ourselves for entire weekends. We spent them mostly in his bed or on his couch, phones silenced and ignored, watching movie after movie, always touching. We paused to eat and to talk in bursts.

We also paused to make love, different from our scrambling, urgent fucking, slower and somehow deeper. On these weekends Dutch grew quieter and more reflective.

"Do you want to go out?" he sometimes asked.

"No," I told him. "This is where I want to be."

Our contentment formed a seal around us, pressing us to each other. These weekends reassured me that whatever we were at the bar together, we were also something else.

Sober, he still needed me close, though the need became more measured, like oxygen rationed in confinement. Alcohol seemed to release him from that small space, allowing him to take giant gulps of air instead of careful sips.

"I love you." Sober, these words came infrequently and in a panic-twinged rush. Drunk, they poured out as freely as bourbon into a glass.

"Do you?"

"I love you," he repeated. "It's you. I know it's you."

I returned sweeping, helpless love. And when he was sober the next day and had again stepped back into himself, I longed for the return of the Dutch I'd glimpsed and held the night before. Part of me naively believed I could and would eventually find a way to access all of him, without alcohol. Part of me guiltily preferred him just to keep drinking, since that was when he loved me most.

But while alcohol made him seek and embrace me, it could also usher in a darkness, out of nowhere. Minor inconveniences triggered wildly disproportionate furies.

One night at a new restaurant in town, the server took too long bringing our drinks. When she spilled a few drops as she set them on the table, Dutch stood so abruptly that he tipped his chair. I righted it, scurried after him out of the restaurant, and didn't hear from him again till the following night.

He asked me to golf with him one bright, warm afternoon. He played and waited patiently as I hacked at the tee, and he let me drive the cart, both of us laughing, yelling, and spilling our beers as we lurched and bumped around the course. His game was going well.

Near the end, his swing got sloppy. He started missing easy shots. I sagged when I saw the darkness descend on him, our beautiful day then over. I was learning to be reactive, to watch for the darkness, to measure and modulate my responses to it.

After missing one shot, he sent his club sailing into the nearby pond with a sudden, powerful wrench of his arm.

"I can't believe you just did that," I gasped.

He said nothing.

Even as a young child I would never have dared such petulance, knowing how swiftly it would have been beaten from me. "Why did you do that?" I faltered.

"Because it's fucking useless. Come on, let's go."

I stared at the pond that had swallowed the club. "How much did that cost?"

"About five hundred," he said curtly. "It doesn't matter. Let's go."

Trailing after him, I looked over my shoulder at the pond one last time. At the bottom of it, I saw the groceries I needed and my unpaid bills. Dutch didn't call me for the next three days.

The reach of the blackness extended beyond inadequate servers and inanimate objects. When he was very drunk, he sometimes clutched me and said, over and over again, "What a piece of shit."

I waited. I had learned to wait.

Over and over again, he circled back to three events, one being Andy's death. "Andy died," he slurred. "Did I ever tell you about my friend Andy?"

"I know about Andy."

"Did I ever tell you that the drive between our houses was five minutes? He dropped me off. He should have been home five minutes later. Five minutes. But he *died. I* almost died. I was sitting right next to him. Did I tell you that?"

I nodded and swallowed hard.

"He was good at school, good at sports. He was nice to girls. He was a nice kid. He wanted to go to college and try to do something. I never wanted to do anything." He swayed before me, stricken and incredulous. "And he *died.* He was just a kid. We were just kids. It should have been me. Almost was. What a piece of shit."

The second event was his accident and trial. "Everybody hated me," he repeated. "I mean, they already did, after Andy. But this clinched it. They hated me. Everybody knew, the whole town. I'd lived there my whole life."

"They didn't hate you." I tried to pull him from the darkness. "It was an accident. It wasn't your fault."

"It doesn't matter. That's what all those people think of when they see me. And I'm stuck with this record forever. It's gonna follow me forever."

He never specifically mentioned the girl, so I didn't either.

The third event he illuminated by saying simply, "I fucking hate him."

I held him and felt my uselessness. "I know."

"Who just leaves their kid? Who can do that?"

I didn't know what to say.

Dutch barreled on, his voice rising. "You know what's hilarious?"

"What's hilarious?" I asked weakly.

"After Andy died, his dad wanted to die. All he wanted was to see his kid again. But *my* dad? I can't get my dad to send a fucking birthday card. And that"—he punched his headboard three times for emphasis—"is. Fucking. Hilarious. Don't you think? I mean, if someone can just leave their kid, what does that say?"

"Nothing about you," I insisted. "Some people are just—broken."

"I'm never, *ever* having kids." He said it many times. And because these declarations were about his sorrow, I pushed away my own and tried to be a bowl.

I had invited Dutch into every corner of my life, and he had included me in his bar circle. I never knew if he'd made a conscious decision about this inclusion or if, because we went to the bar together so often, he had simply resigned himself to it. But other parts of his life remained opaque. Some nights he was strangely vague about his plans, and only if pressed would he offer names I'd never or rarely heard him mention before.

One morning in bed, his phone rang. Normally he let it go to voicemail or took the call lying next to me. This time, he sprang out of bed as he answered.

"Hey… Good, man. You ready for tonight?"

He hurried out of the bedroom. I heard the click of the bathroom door closing.

"I'll be there around four."

I heard him turn on the faucet.

"You got 'em? How many?"

I sat up in bed, straining to hear.

"All right, good. Yeah, it'll be a good time. All right. All right."

When I heard him end the call and turn off the water, I lay down again.

"Who was that?" I asked when he returned.

"Jimmy. A friend from home. I'm heading back for a couple days."

"Today?"

"Yeah."

"Oh." He hadn't mentioned it. I watched as he pulled on a T-shirt. "What are you guys gonna do?"

"Just party a little bit. That's the usual deal." He pulled on some jeans. "Wanna go out for breakfast?"

"Sure." I hesitated. "What's he getting for you?"

"What?"

"You asked him if he's got them." I started getting dressed.

"Oh." He looked around for his phone and wallet. "I wanted to make sure he's got his clubs. We might golf."

"At night?"

"No." He gave me a quizzical smile. "Tomorrow. Are you ready? I'm starving."

I paced in his absence, unsettled that I barely heard from him and that he hadn't told me sooner about this trip. That he hadn't invited me this time or any other injured me in ways I struggled more and more to conceal. My mind kept drifting back to the phone call I had partially overheard.

He returned cheerful, pulling me into him. We went out and laughed through the night. I came three times. We slept curled against each other as always, and the next morning, I heard him whistling in the shower. *He's right here.* Still, the edginess would not leave me.

I eyed the duffel bag he'd dropped near the front door after his trip. *You got 'em? How many?* After a quick calculation of how much longer he'd be in the shower, I sprang at the bag and rifled through it.

Under some clothes, I found a Ziploc bag holding about a

hundred pills, all of them white, in different shapes and sizes.

Hearing the shower stop, I tucked the Ziploc back beneath the clothes, rezipped the duffel bag, and hurried back to the couch. By the time Dutch came down the stairs, I had carefully arranged my face in neutral.

I needed to think. I needed the right moment. It presented itself when he said he was going out for the night with someone else I'd never heard of, someone named Chris. When I answered the call from an unknown number the next morning, it was Dutch, saying he'd borrowed someone's phone and needed a ride.

"Where are you?" I asked groggily.

He gave me the address. When I pulled up in front of the unfamiliar house, he emerged pale and sweaty, both exhausted and frenetic. He directed me to another house I'd never been to, where he retrieved his phone, and finally to the parking lot where his car sat. As we drove, he tried to relay the previous night's events, which included Chris's cocaine.

Before he got into his car, I put mine in park. "You look awful."

"I feel awful." When he leaned toward me, I held up my hand to stop him.

"It's caked all over your *nostrils*, Dutch."

He rubbed frantically at his nose in the visor mirror. I twisted toward him. "What are you doing?"

"I don't know. I fucked up."

Tell him. "You know, I found pills in your bag."

He looked sick.

"This is crazy." I shook my head. "You have to stop this."

He said he knew that. He agreed, and said he would. He called it "a bad run," one he hadn't had in a long time, and wouldn't again. He said, almost pleading, "Don't hate me."

"Just—please stop. You have to stop."

This time when he tried to hug me, I reciprocated.

In *Walk the Line*, at one of the lowest points of his addiction, Johnny Cash tumbled down a wooded hill to the muddy waters below. Seeing this, torn over whether or not to go to him, June said to her mother, "If I go down there—"

Her mother interrupted her. "You already are down there, honey."

I was. Not in the mud, but in the car, quietly tangled across the center console, my hands passing over Dutch's back. It was as if death were written on him.

No. Here, the ropey hardness of his arms. Here, the span of his shoulders. Here, the physical space he took up, the solidity of him. *He's right here.* My presence, I thought then, forced the darkness he had stumbled into to recede.

At the bar only weeks later, my presence made no difference. He started talking to a group of people neither of us had ever seen before. Their conversation turned to pills. They were looking to buy.

"I've got some," he told them in a low voice. "Come check it out if you want."

My stomach churned. He wouldn't look at me. They readily agreed to come back to his house.

Soon, the skunked, pungent air of his house made me gag. Strangers with faces like wolves dotted the first floor. Several congregated around Dutch, sitting on his couch, bent over his coffee table. This place, which had become as comfortable and familiar to me as my own apartment, suddenly felt foreign.

Later that night I went looking for Dutch and found him upstairs, on his bed, out cold.

I kicked everyone out and locked the door. As I carried an armful of empty bottles to the kitchen, I lingered on the photo stuck to the fridge, one I had looked at many times. It showed Dutch with his mom and extended family at their last large gathering, all with arms resting across one another's shoulders, all smiling. The juxtaposition of the wholesome picture with this night created a cloying stickiness on my skin.

Leaning in to study June more closely, I again felt the pull of affinity. We both tried to love men away from some precipice where they perpetually hovered. And without meaning to, intending only to do her best for her son, June had strapped skates to Dutch's feet and given him a push.

All that money. I searched June's face. *It was the worst thing you could have done.*

The next morning, I was picking up the living room when Dutch appeared, shivering and clutching a blanket around himself. "Why did you open the windows?"

"Because it stinks in here." I crisscrossed the room, restoring its order. "Why did you let people smoke weed in your house?"

"Because." He stumbled to the kitchen for a glass of water. "I'm opening a glaucoma clinic."

When he returned and settled gingerly on the couch, I faced him. "Since when are you selling pills?"

"They're not mine." He took a long, shaky sip of water. "I'm helping out a friend, one time."

"What friend?"

I watched him deliberate as he sipped. "Jimmy."

I filed the name away. He regarded me over the rim of his glass in silence.

"What does he need your help for?" I paused. "And why does he think you *can* help him, or that you would?"

But Dutch had easily dispensed the pills in one night with strangers. I realized it as soon as I asked the question.

When he ignored it, I shook my head. "I don't understand you." The last time he'd been remorseful, and fearful that I would leave. This time, he was almost daring me.

What had he said once? With him, there was always a next time.

"I don't understand why you're doing this. It's like you *want* something bad to happen."

"Nothing bad is happening."

"You could have been robbed last night. You didn't know *any* of those people, and you just left them in your house and went to *sleep*. With this all over the place." Disgusted, I waved an arm over the weed and pills and cash scattered across the coffee table. "Jesus, they could have rolled a moving van up and taken the TVs off the walls and you wouldn't have known."

"Okay." He banged his glass down on the coffee table. "Stop lecturing me."

"I'm trying to—"

"No. Don't try to do anything. You're not my guidance counselor. I'm not your fucking project."

I resumed my angry cleaning.

"And stop cleaning." He stood. "This isn't your house. This is *my* house, last time I checked."

I dropped my arms to my sides. "You want me to go?"

"I want you to go."

That time, he was gone for a week.

Limping through his absences, I came to realize how often I misjudged Dutch and our relationship. I'd thought that my presence somehow safeguarded him. I'd thought that while he turned on himself and others, he would not turn on me. For a while, I had remained untouched by the darkness except as a witness, and I'd believed that love made me exempt. Then he began criticizing my appearance.

The first time he did it, the first time anyone I'd dated had ever done that to me, I felt like I'd been struck.

Afterward, I tried in my stammering, fumbling way to dismiss it as an aberration. It became impossible.

When on a walk together and I slid out of my flip-flops to feel the warm sidewalk beneath my bare feet: "Are you a guest on the Jerry Springer Show today?" When driving to dinner: "Is your hair supposed to look like that?" When I hopped into his car wearing jeans and a faded denim jacket: "Are we going to a Whitesnake concert?" The impact was almost physical.

On a Friday night, I stopped by his house before heading out with Claire and Fiona. Glancing at me, Dutch said, "You only dress up for them. You never look this good for me." The welts rose instantly. The next night, I made painstaking preparations to see him, changing six times. He surveyed me with chilly detachment. "All black, huh? Are we going to a funeral?"

A funeral. It wasn't that, a singular ritual of finality. This was entering the water, unthinking and languid at first, then looking back at the beach, the shock of realizing how far out I'd been drawn.

When I first glided into Dutch's line of sight, I'd lacked any instinct to edit or second-guess myself. In return, he had made me feel boundlessly, expansively interesting and electrically fuckable. *Look at my girlfriend.* I never forgot him saying that, or how he had looked at me the night I wore the pink dress.

Do I look different now? I searched and searched my reflection for answers, expecting to find them. When we slept together, I began to wake first, jolted by a panicky internal alarm. At the cottage, the first sliver of pale gray light on the lake drove me out of bed to the bathroom.

After a shower and a furtive peek around the corner to ensure he was still asleep, I put on a new bikini, pale blush to accentuate my tan. Then I stood back and studied myself in the slightly fogged full-length mirror.

I stepped forward, scrutinizing. I stepped back and turned. In one moment, my lines looked long and lean. In the next, my thighs touched. My breasts looked full, my stomach flat. Then, they sagged. I looked like someone who belonged in this place, with him. Then, my entire body bloated and rippled with excess. Forward, back, turn. My reflection changed continuously like the color and texture of the lake.

I stared into the mirror. *How am I back here?* Maybe I'd been here all along, still thrashing in waters I only thought I had escaped. The prospect of the beach filled me with dread.

I could, I thought, step out into the sun one way and then, by bending the wrong way or standing the wrong way or angling my body the wrong way, I could transform in an instant, and before Dutch's very eyes, into someone with no business in a bikini on a beach.

I remembered a story an old friend had told me. In high school, her bulimia had landed her in therapy, and in one group session, each girl had taken a turn lying on a large piece of paper on the floor while the others traced her outline.

The image made me shudder. "What for?"

"To understand your body dysmorphia," she explained. "You see yourself one way in your mind, but then the drawing shows you how the rest of the world sees you. It's supposed to be revelatory."

I couldn't have conceived of a worse hell. But that morning with Dutch, I would have done it in an instant if it meant not having to face the beach.

We walked it, surveying the horizon together. The lake was a mirror.

Dutch shielded his eyes with his hand. "Want to try for those sandbars now?"

There, just within reach, they sparkled in the sunlight. "Let's do it."

"Stop." His tone arced, teasing. "There's no way."

I faced him. "You didn't think I'd be able to throw or catch a baseball properly, and I could. You didn't think I'd be able to keep up with you on the bikes, and I could. I'll prove you wrong about this too."

"Yeah?" He cocked his head. I lifted my chin. "Okay. If you say so."

He peeled off the T-shirt protecting his scorched shoulders and plunged into the water. I followed.

Dutch's arms and legs sliced so easily through the water that he left me behind almost immediately. I swam hard to catch up, caught off guard by the size of the waves, my chest tightening when I saw him waiting at the first sandbar. Standing, his shoulders hardly cleared the surface. When I arrived, I could barely touch the bottom.

"Jesus." I tried to steady my breath, to smile at him, to bounce so the swells wouldn't wash over me. Each one forced more water into my mouth. "This is a lot farther than it looks."

"Two to go. Come on." He was off.

I flung myself forward. The shore got farther and farther away, but the destination seemed no closer. I thrashed and thrashed.

When I reached the second sandbar, he was waiting, treading water that would have covered our heads by several feet. I lunged for his neck, wrapping my arms around it, looking back at the shore. It looked hopelessly, desolately distant.

"I'm going back." I clung to him.

"We're almost there."

"No, you were right. I give. Let's go back."

"We're almost there." And just before he broke away from me, I felt my insignificance in this churn. What a wonder, I thought as I bobbed in it, to feel so small.

He headed for the third sandbar. I was sinking. Panic propelled me upward and back toward the shore.

I beat my pulpy arms and legs against the water. My chest heaved. My lungs strained. One more push, one more burst of frantic effort, carried me in.

I dropped to the sand, panting. When he returned, we sat side by side on the beach, listening to each other's breathing slow to normal. We watched the lake glitter in the sun.

"You okay?" Dutch asked.

My panic subsided. I tried not to cry and considered apologizing.

He stood, took my hands, and pulled me to my feet. "Come on. Let's get a drink."

6

Glick's party started with about twenty people, then swelled, then dwindled as the night wore on. Eventually eight of us, including Dutch and me, sat around a bonfire in the backyard. Again I found myself the only woman, and again my transformative powers took hold.

I could become a bowl. I could, by adjusting my gait and eye contact and hair so that it tumbled over my shoulders, magnetize myself. When I did this, I saw how men's eyes moved over my body.

I could stand in front of my students and pass for an academic. I made myself look and sound like someone who was qualified and competent at the lectern.

I could also, in groups of men like this, fade into them so that they talked in front of me as if I weren't there. Someone asked Glick about the woman, gone by then, who'd hovered smiling at his side most of the night.

"I don't know, man." He added a log to the fire. "I just met her. She's all right, but"—he jabbed at the flames with a stick—"she's not that hot."

I stiffened. General agreement circled the group, and then it was my turn.

I wanted to say that I'd found the woman perfectly pretty in a freshly scrubbed, churchy way. I wanted to say that every time I saw Glick lately, his stomach seemed to sag more over his jeans, and that the sticky substance he put in his hair to make it youthfully messy didn't conceal the expanding ring of baldness. I wanted to condemn this collective judgment of a woman's appearance.

I said, "We can't help who we're attracted to, right?" More consensus followed. A voice inside me whispered, *Judas.*

Glick shrugged noncommittally as he finished his beer.

"Probably not gonna turn into anything."

Dutch rose to refill his drink. As he walked away, he said over his shoulder, "Yeah, man. Can't let a girl lower your stock."

Again I remembered what Dutch had said long ago. *It's one thing to understand, to believe. It's another to actually be different.*

I understood. I believed. I had also just sold out a woman to remain in good standing with a bunch of aging frat boys. Sitting there in that circle, I felt my complicity and hated myself.

The men I'd grown up around viewed all women—and especially *their* women, because their feeling was proprietary—as Fabergé eggs, meant to be admired and handled with great care. As a result, I had always vocalized my contempt for men who mistreated women, particularly when they dated my girlfriends. I'd told them, full of sincere and resounding and appropriate outrage, "You're too good for him. He doesn't deserve you. You don't need this shit."

I had believed my upbringing and my feminism inoculated me against such offenses. And still, there I stood in the dark, my ribcage knocking hollowly, wanting only to be back in the light.

I had long since stopped telling Claire and Fiona everything, instead revealing only bits and pieces, balanced out by positive anecdotes, and only in case of emergency. This felt like an emergency.

The next time we convened, I didn't give specifics. I didn't tell them what he'd said about lowered stock. I said that lately I'd noticed him focusing on my appearance. That it was bothering me.

Claire's eyes immediately narrowed. "Focusing how? What did he say?"

"It's more a general sense than what he's specifically saying," I lied, then produced a trickle of murky, watery non-narrative. I couldn't and wouldn't fully articulate my troubles. They insulated and isolated me.

Claire leaned back in the booth. Fiona leaned forward. Their eyes landed on my body, trying to discern it beneath my loose-fitting jeans and T-shirt, their look familiar and searching.

We had all been here together before.

At my sickest, some of my male friends' sudden interest in fucking me had disoriented and annoyed me. Some of my female friends had gushed, and some had become jealous. My parents had beamed with pride.

Claire and Fiona had remained quiet, watching and finally confronting me in my bedroom. Claire had given me a long, strange look. Then she pounced, lifting my tank top to reveal the waist, rolled several times to hold my jeans in place. Claire seized the weapon-like angles of my hips.

"This is crazy," she had told me then. I tried to squirm away but she held me. "You have to stop this."

"You have to," Fiona echoed, stepping toward us. "Please. Please stop this."

They both advanced, their arms wrapping me, their hands across my bony back. I must have felt like death was written on me.

They'd been fearful of this when we were teenagers, too fearful to name it or talk about it beyond their repeated entreaties: "Please stop. You have to stop." We had all lacked the right language then. And now in our thirties, we were no more fluent. We looked across the table at each other, helpless.

Claire's voice tightened. "You can't go back there."

"I know. I'm not. I won't."

"You can't be with someone who takes you back there."

"I don't think it's that, exactly." I tried to say something true. "I think a lot of this is me."

"But something about him is bringing this up again."

"I'm really not sure."

"It sounds," Fiona offered, "like you don't know what to do."

"I don't."

"I know what you should do," Claire snorted. "Run."

"Stop," Fiona rebuked her.

But Claire waved her off. "I remember all of that, Fi. Do you?"

"Yes, I remember," Fiona said, exasperated. They moved further into their argument and briefly forgot me. I sipped my beer.

"This is some asshole shit," Claire insisted. "Do you really think she should hang around for someone who takes her back to all that?"

"She didn't say that."

"She didn't need to."

Huffy, Fiona returned to me. "You love him."

"I do."

"Why?" Claire demanded. "What is it?"

I thought then of how I had explained it to Dutch in one of my handwritten letters. I had described a bright fall afternoon in high school when my friend Liz had picked me up in her dad's Corvette, as shiny and red as strawberry lip gloss. I couldn't remember what we talked or laughed about that day. I couldn't remember if we had gone anywhere in particular, or why Liz's dad had lent her the car. That he had granted his sixteen-year-old daughter access to the car had awed me. That he owned such a thing had impressed me. My own dad was far too practical.

I remembered the heady leather interior and the engine, rumbling as we cruised the roads outside of town, roaring when Liz hit the gas. I remembered how the dappled sunlight had played off the windshield, how the trees crowding the hills we wound through had turned gem-colored, how Sting's "Fields of Gold" had drifted from the speakers.

I turned it up. We lowered the windows. I stuck my hand out to ride the current of the air. And every time I looked back on that ride, as I'd done many times through the years, I realized what I'd felt then was sheer joy, the full realization of my youth and its boundless possibility. All my adventures lay gleaming ahead of me.

This, I had concluded in my letter to Dutch, *is exactly how I feel when I'm with you.*

The futility of trying to convey this to Claire fatigued me. I said only, "You don't know him like I do, Claire. No one can look at someone else's relationship and fully see it."

Claire cocked her head. "You don't sound like you."

This is going to hurt. I braced myself.

"You sound like the kind of woman who used to annoy you, the kind who tries to excuse and explain away a man's bad behavior."

Now we had both said something true.

"But you love him," Fiona repeated. "Talk to him about this. Tell him how you feel. He probably doesn't even know." She paused. "Does he know? About you?"

"He does. I mean, I told him, a long time ago. But I'm not sure how much he understands." I finished my beer. "I'm not sure anyone really understands unless they've been through it."

"But maybe he *does* understand," Claire objected. "Maybe he's using your history as ammunition."

"Fuck's sake, Claire, you make him out to be a monster," Fiona snapped. Then she turned to me. "He's a guy. He probably has no idea what's coming up for you."

"Maybe."

"You just need to talk. You can work through this." I could always count on Fiona to champion love. She turned to Claire. "What is it with you? If a relationship isn't perfect, it's a total write-off?"

Claire was agitated. "I don't want our friend to be with someone who makes her feel bad. Do you?"

"Of course not. I'm just saying, maybe if a relationship is important, you work on it. Maybe it's worth the effort."

Claire went to the bar for the next round and returned chewing her lip, thinking. Then, "You know, we saw him."

"We who? Him who?"

"We." Claire gestured at herself and Fiona, who shot her a look that was impossible to misunderstand. *We said we weren't going to tell her.* "And James, and everyone. We all went out a couple weeks ago, the night you said you had to grade papers. We saw Dutch."

Claire looked so stiff, and Fiona so flustered, that I immediately broke into a cold sweat. The words wobbled when I said them. "You saw him with a woman?"

"No, nothing like that," Fiona said quickly.

Claire continued, "We were all there first, at Hurley's. And when he showed up—"

"With a couple guys," Fiona interjected.

"When he showed up, we waved," Claire went on. "I thought he'd come over or we'd all go over to him. We'd all just hung out the week before, and we had a good time, remember?"

"I remember." When I asked him to join me and my friends, Dutch always said no. I stopped asking. The night Claire was talking about, his request to come along had astounded me.

"Yes. Of course. Please," I'd said. "They want to know you better."

Several times that night, looking at my boyfriend and my friends, crowded around one large table, laughing and talking, I had flushed with pleasure.

But on the night Claire meant, when I had stayed home to grade, "He didn't wave back. I thought maybe he didn't see us, so I waved again."

"And?"

"And nothing. He just turned around, back to the guys he came with."

My face warmed. I tried to picture it. "Is it possible that he really didn't see you?"

"He saw us," Claire said.

"But people don't always want to talk all the time, which is fine," Fiona added with characteristic charity.

We fell into a rare awkward silence.

In my mind I replayed the night Dutch had joined us. He had asked to come. He had reciprocated my friends' easy warmth. He had seemed happy.

I said all I could think to say. "I'll talk to him."

As Dutch and I settled into bed the next night, I ventured, "Did you see my friends out a couple weeks ago?"

"I did." He searched for the remote. "I didn't tell you?"

"No." I adjusted the pillows, stalling. "Why did you pretend not to see them?"

Part of me expected him to lash out. Instead, he apologized. He had been so drunk, he said, embarrassingly drunk.

"Oh." He was sorry. It was over. "You were at a bar, though." Perplexed, I pressed a little further. "Everyone was probably drunk. *They* were probably drunk. What's to be embarrassed about?"

"I just didn't want to look like an asshole in front of your friends."

"You didn't want to look like an asshole in front of my friends…" I spoke carefully. "So you turned your back and pretended not to see them."

"Okay." He paused. "But if I was drunk and they were drunk, everyone was drunk, it doesn't really matter. Does it?"

I flashed to the previous night's silence with Claire and Fiona, the three of us equally mystified by this snub, equally disconcerted by this new, small tear in our sisterhood. It mattered.

But here lay Dutch, in bed and me beside him, wanting to be nowhere else. It mattered.

He repeated, "I'm sorry." We both hesitated. Then he clicked on the TV and gathered me to him.

When Dutch wounded me or shoved me away, I closed in on myself, a skill that didn't come naturally. I practiced and built up defenses. When I felt fortified enough to withstand his alienation, he pulled me close again, jarring me, like when he asked me to go to Memphis.

"Memphis?" We stood in his kitchen, salting the rims of our margaritas. I dropped a hunk of lime into mine. "What's happening in Memphis?"

His entire extended family convened once a year. That year, a cousin had volunteered his sprawling property for the gathering. "And so I thought," he continued, "that maybe you could come."

"Oh." June was the only family member I'd met, and I knew that meeting was a significant exception. "Do you think they would mind me being there? Your family?"

"No, they want to meet you. They know about you. I told them you'd probably come." He said this all in a rush. "Not that you have to. You'd have to meet everyone all at once, and then, you know, deal with them for a whole week. It's a lot. But, if you're into it…" He exhaled. "What do you think? Want to go?"

"I do." I smiled. "You know I've always wanted to go there. Go walking in Memphis, like the song?"

He relaxed a little. "That's a great song."

"Yeah." My smile widened. "'Elvis, catfish, gospel—I want all of that.'"

He objected, "You would never eat catfish."

"I wouldn't. But I want it *on the table*."

He booked two seats. Then we carried our margaritas out to his deck and sat in the dwindling twilight, watching as the fireflies brought the backyard to colored, blinking life.

When he reached toward me like this, the tenderness of his reach seemed to reveal him. I relaxed and unfolded again like paper. I reached back. Then he swatted me away again, jarring me.

Like when I took him to the Mexican restaurant, a place near campus that the faculty and I frequented. The hostess seated us by a table of men I knew from the English department. I said hello. I forgot. We ate.

As we left, Dutch said, "So that's what you're into."

I looked at him, my face blank.

"You know, guys like that." He jerked his head toward the restaurant. Irascibility distorted his features. "Academics. That's what you're into."

Before I could formulate a response, a group of girls crossed our path, hurrying, giggling girls with swinging salon hair and spiked heels, all poreless and flawless, all cleavage and long, bare legs.

"That's fine." He gestured at the girls. "Because that's what *I'm* into."

I could never predict or prevent these bursts of venom, the kind that instantly ruined everything, the kind that seemed to reveal him. What a wonder, I thought as we returned to the car in silence, to feel so small.

The coexistence of wrath and love in Dutch confounded me. Which was weightier, I couldn't see. Whether he was most himself when he cut me or when he clung to me, I couldn't tell. I couldn't understand the truth of him.

He'd told me that his dating roster had included lots of hairstylists, personal trainers, and bartenders. He'd told me that he liked that I taught Aristotle and Marx, that books stacked the surfaces in my apartment, that sometimes when he stopped by, he'd find classical music soaring in the air and me bent over a stack of papers. He'd told his mom and his friends that I was different. But if my education was a virtue, it also posed a threat.

Since finishing grad school, I'd been an adjunct. I'd thrown elbows every few months to secure teaching assignments at three different colleges, racing between them to make class on time and to make rent, scraping along and never knowing my fate from semester to semester. One night after finishing a mind-numbing stretch of grading, I clicked on a show called *Divorce*. In it, a teen compared adjuncts teaching college courses to hospital janitors performing surgery.

"Fuck *you*," I said to the TV.

Adjuncts like me taught the courses that full-time faculty would not. We taught more of them at a time for a fraction of the pay, and we did it without health insurance or job security. I belonged to an impoverished army doing the majority of the actual teaching at large institutions, while the money saved on us flowed instead toward gleaming new athletic facilities and impressive salaries for tenured professors.

But then one day, the Catholic university where I taught posted a full-time position. I applied, interviewed, and got the job. Dutch and I went out to celebrate.

At the bar I told friends about the new job. "The salary's pretty humble." But for the first time, I told them, I'd have a steady income and a reasonable schedule. I would no longer need to scramble every few months to remain employed. I could go to the doctor if I needed to. "And I get my own office, which is downright luxurious. No more grading papers in my car."

Clever bought me a beer. Glick said he'd pick up the next one. Kevin said, "That's great news."

"It *is* great," Dutch said. In his tone, I heard a now familiar warning.

"Yeah, man." Kevin's voice trailed off.

"Those degrees are finally paying off," Dutch continued, getting louder, taking a long pull from his drink, another pink Clever creation. The last one had made him jovial. This one had brought on the darkness. "You got your dream job, teaching morons their shapes and colors."

Heat rushed to my face. Everyone shifted on their barstools.

Glick tried to help by belittling his own girlfriend. "Dude, Alexis' job is to wipe sweat off the machines at the gym," he offered with a weak laugh. "So…this sounds like a pretty good deal."

"It's great, like I said." Dutch raised his glass toward Glick as if to toast. "Now your girl and my girl will be making about the same amount of money."

"Take it easy, man," someone muttered. Someone else cleared his throat. Kevin asked, "What's going on with this game?" We lifted our collective gaze to the TV.

When I slipped out the back door a few minutes later, I heard my name and turned. Clever leaned against the wall, smoking a cigarette.

"Heading out?"

"Yeah." I was done with banter.

"Okay." He looked jumpy. "You know, I probably shouldn't be saying this, but—" He stopped himself and looked toward the back door as he drew on his cigarette. I waited. "I think you're a good one."

My eyes narrowed. *Are you hitting on me?*

"I think you're a good person." Again he looked toward the door. "And you deserve good things. You know?"

He wasn't hitting on me. He was committing treason.

He dropped his cigarette. "Take care of yourself." Without waiting for a response, he hurried back inside.

The next day, I didn't respond to Dutch's calls or texts. When he showed up at my door, he sat bleary-eyed on my couch as I recounted the previous night. He remembered almost none of it.

Maybe I could explain my injury, I thought, and he could heal it. Maybe I could explain that he had inflicted it, and he would stop. I tried.

"You said you were proud of me…that I'm smart, that I got this job…"

His face, his entire being, hardened before my eyes.

"But last night, you made me feel worthless…"

He cut me off.

"You did it in front of everyone… You humiliated me…"

He left.

I dragged myself through the first few days of punishing silence, now accustomed to it. I withered as the silence stretched into weeks. I waited, a skill he had forced me to master. My training dictated that in his presence, I should expect his departure, and in his absence, I should expect his return.

But this time, he wasn't coming back.

7

After four years, we ended our romantic relationship. This decision was mutual, amicable, and unrelated to drugs or alcohol.

He ended our relationship several times over the course of four years, abruptly each time, spinning on his heel and walking away while my unfinished sentence dangled in the air.

When he left for good, taking his sunlight with him, the immediacy and density of the engulfing darkness stunned me. I didn't know how to move in it. The pain, indistinguishable from a physical affliction, immobilized me.

"Are you saying you want to die?" On the phone, I heard the anxious pinch in Fiona's voice.

"No. I don't want to die." My voice was thick with snot. "I'm saying I feel like I *am* dying, actively dying. Like I need a doctor."

I lay curled on my couch, sure that something could and must be done about the pain.

"He loves me, he loves me, he loves me," I told Fiona. "And all of the sudden he's just—gone. No discussion, no sadness, no emotion at all. It's been this way every time."

The final time had gutted me.

I had waited out a week. Finally, I'd called him, telling him when he answered, "I'm coming over." He didn't tell me not to. I found the door unlocked when I arrived.

He was sitting on his couch, mute and expressionless. His detachment was as complete as it was, for me, catastrophic.

"Dutch," I'd implored him. "It's me." I'd said it again and again. He remained unmoved, unmovable.

Finally, I'd advanced, knelt in front of him, and placed my hands on his knees, hoping my touch would make a difference. "Dutch."

My shaking, shattered presence hardly registered.

Fiona asked, "Do you think he was drunk?"

"He wasn't." I knew well how that pendulum swung between tenderness and malice. I would have welcomed either. "He just has this switch. And when he flips it, that's it."

Before Dutch, I couldn't remember when I had last cried. When tears threatened, my inner Marine had barked at me, steeled me. Now, if not moving woodenly through classes or groups of strangers in public, I cried all the time, prompted by the silence of my apartment, the vastness of my bed, a memory, the assault of sunshine, a song playing in a store, or nothing at all. My formerly sturdy exterior thinned to little more than a membrane, quick to perforate and puncture.

I fled from music and movies and books, all of them minefields. Eventually I settled on two relatively safe spaces, one being NPR, the drone of it anesthetizing me as I drove to work or drank coffee in my kitchen.

The other was murder shows, which I clicked on each night. They played on and on as I drifted off into fitful sleep on my couch.

"Are you saying they *soothe* you?" my friends asked, laughing a little, trying to gauge how worried they should be.

"They don't make me feel better," I tried to explain. "But they don't make me feel worse."

The shows almost never depicted love or happiness, or if they did, only fleetingly, as a deceptive precursor to inevitable tragedy. I appreciated their grayness, the ominous soundtracks, the starkness of police interrogation rooms. They matched my own interior.

The shows often told stories of people who had initially gone missing, for weeks or months or even years. In interviews their family members all described a sense of suspension in their anguish, of hovering in it. The space previously occupied by their loved one opened into a vacuous absence, most likely a death. But they all said, their faces etched by suffering, that without confirmation, without a body and a grave to visit, "Part of you is always waiting for them to walk through the door."

Yes. I sat in the darkness, blinking at the TV, my own etched face washed in its ghostly light. *It's exactly like that.*

My parents fretted. Fiona started showing up unannounced to take me on little excursions. During a trip to the farmer's market, she guided me past the stalls, a gentle aide with her shuffling charge, loading her arms with pink flowers.

I nodded at them when we returned to my apartment. "Better get those home and into some water."

"They're for you," she sang. Inside, she rummaged through my kitchen for vases and pitchers, which she filled and placed on empty surfaces.

"There," she said when she'd finished. She looked so hopeful. "Nice and cheerful."

When Claire arrived a few minutes later, she dropped a case of beer on the counter and looked around at the flowers. "Damn. Who died?"

Away from the sunlight of the farmer's market, now entombed in my apartment, the bursts of pink looked garish and funereal. *We died.*

My pack did what had always worked before and hauled me to Ginty's, where James could usually be found behind the bar, holding court. Our beloved, somewhat exasperating friend took far too long to summarize movies and his views on UFOs and conspiracy theories, monologues Claire called his "staircases to nowhere." He was also a menace to women. We had lectured him many times about his bad behavior.

But we loved him and his stories. This one, which he told leaning over the bar toward us, involved a woman named Janice who'd come into the pub a week earlier.

She was older, he told us, in her late forties but "very well maintained." He took her home. When Janice returned the next night, she brought a group of women. "I think she wanted to show me off."

Most of the women with her had appeared roughly her age, but one looked much younger. James wondered if he should card her. Instead, he flirted with her when Janice went to the bathroom. He took her home.

On the third night, Janice and the younger woman returned together, furious after discovering that James had had sex with both of them. They were mother and daughter.

"James." Fiona covered her face. "You're such a... *bartender.*"

Everyone laughed. I excused myself to cry in the bathroom.

Afterward, I gripped the sides of the sink and stared in disbelief at the puffy, crumpled face looking back at me in the mirror.

I slipped out the back door without saying goodbye to anyone, a new move which made my friends exchange glances, and which I began employing when they got me out at all. James started calling me Houdini.

Claire tried scolding me out of my grief. "You're not coming now?" I waved her away when she came to collect me for an agreed-upon outing. "Why won't you come?"

"I can't do this tonight. I thought I could but I can't."

She flopped onto the couch, exasperated. For years, we'd been knights who'd clanked around in matching armor and in agreement on the importance of dignified suffering, conducted as privately and expeditiously as possible.

"I know you don't realize this right now"—I braced myself for what came next—"but you dodged a bullet. You're lucky."

The twitter that escaped me sounded deranged. *Lucky.*

"I mean it, you have to stop this." Claire rose from the couch. I thought she might shake me. "You have to get it together."

"Well, shit, Claire. Show me where that button is and I'll push it."

We faced each other, almost angry. She was still a knight. I was now a burn victim, every nerve exposed.

Months of solitude dragged by. I did little else but work, and that only technically. Someone resembling me still showed up to class, moving through material I hadn't prepared, assigning papers and eventually returning them with a score scrawled on the first page.

Jerrod, one of my favorite students, tried to bolster sagging classroom morale by cracking jokes, asking on Mondays about my weekend, and injecting comments like we were friends. We might have been, if he weren't a teenager.

During a brief pause in my lecture, he noted, "You know, you play with that ring all the time."

"I know." I shuffled through a pile of papers to redirect my hands. I couldn't take off the ring.

I avoided student conferences, skipped meetings, and waited to be reprimanded.

Nine months after the breakup, I was driving home from work when I remembered I had used the last of my bread and peanut butter for breakfast that morning. Having no other food in my apartment, I decided to stop at Ginty's and hang out with James while I waited for takeout.

This minor detour, I thought as I pulled into the parking lot, might be less terrible than going straight home to face the silence. I made decisions this way now. No good or better option existed. I simply tried to make the least terrible choice.

James grinned when I walked in. "Hey. Anybody coming up?"

"No, I'm just getting some food to go."

He slid a plastic menu across the bar to me. "Why don't you eat here and hang out with me? It's slow." The evening crowd had not yet materialized. Only a few old-timers and regulars dotted the normally busy pub.

I wavered. James felt like a spot of warmth in the cold. But here again I felt that familiar pit in my stomach, that creeping fear of the other patrons turning to watch me eat. *She shouldn't be eating that.* I said, "No, I've got to get home and do some grading."

"All right." He put in my order, brought me a beer I didn't ask for, checked on the regulars, and returned. "So what's the craic?"

Our chats adhered to the mundane, a marker of our friendship that I appreciated. He didn't see what women saw, or pretended not to. He obliged if I wanted to go to the bar or play pool or play cards instead of getting into a lot of talk. This was his preference.

He stepped away to answer the phone and returned with a glass and dishtowel in hand. "Are you seeing anyone these days?"

I bent my head at him. "Are you serious?"

He blinked. "What?"

"James." I almost laughed.

"What?"

"You've been around these last nine months."

"Yeah?" He dried the glass.

"You know what's going on. I've been in the bell jar."

He grabbed more glasses from a steaming rack beneath the bar. "I don't know what that means."

"I barely even pass for human anymore. You've hung out with me. You know what's going on. How could I possibly be seeing anyone?" His question irritated me, like a transplant patient asked if she was training for any upcoming triathlons.

"I just wondered if you were getting back out there. That's all."

James, I remembered then, really missed so much. And while our friendship was sometimes so refreshing, it also sometimes felt like a friendship with a seventeen-year-old boy.

I wondered when my food would appear. "I know you don't have much of an attention span, but we're not wired like that."

"Who's *we*? Girls?"

"Women."

His smile was small. "I have more of an attention span than you think."

I snorted. "Since when?"

"Well." He dried the glasses slowly. "I guess since I met Fiona."

I stared at him, not understanding, and he met my gaze,

smiling again in a way that seemed terribly sad. *Fiona.* We'd all been friends for so many years. James had been right there with us through all of her boyfriends. She'd talked about them to James, or in front of him, and he had said all the wrong things and cracked stupid jokes that made everyone laugh. Fiona had laughed too, and then shaken her head. Our sweet friend James.

I looked at him. "Did you ever tell her?"

"Once, a few years ago." He shrugged, his face bland. "She was really nice about it, just said she didn't feel the same way and cared about me and hoped we'd always be friends. You know the speech. And we all got so drunk that night that I just played it off later."

He tossed the dish towel on the bar. "And now she's with Denny, so."

So.

I ventured, "Is that hard?"

"Of course. But she seems pretty into him, and he seems like a good guy. A bit like watching paint dry"—I laughed—"but a good guy." He shrugged again. "What can you do? That's it."

"But it's right there in front of you all the time. How do you stand it?"

"What can you do?" he repeated. "There's nothing you can do. Time for other fish and all that shit. Unless you want to stay in the…what did you call it? Bell curve?"

"Bell jar."

"That's it."

When he brought me the white bag sitting in the kitchen window, I felt through the plastic that its contents had gone cold. I stood and paid and hugged him.

"Other fish," he called as I headed out the door. I held a hand up without looking back.

Fiona. James missed a lot, but I realized now that I had too.

I had never perceived any difference in the way he treated Fiona, Claire, or me. I had never noticed a seam opening between him and Fiona, or sensed that she was carrying a secret. That she had withheld it threw me. But really, it made so much sense. Fiona would have thought of James's feelings. She would not have betrayed him.

In the days that followed, I kept thinking about the difference between me and James. He didn't hide at home. He didn't cry in bathrooms. He proceeded. My inability these last months to proceed, even to try to stop the bleeding, suddenly infuriated me. The new presence of anger, of any emotion other than crushing sadness, came as a welcome surprise and a relief.

I decided to venture out to the bar. I would begin my restoration.

As I walked, I remembered that Dutch, or any of our mutual friends, might *be* there. I considered every bar in town one of "our" spots, and the possibility of an encounter made my heart hammer in my chest. I almost turned around.

It was kind of like a divorce, I thought with a bitter little smile. Only instead of dividing custody and assets, we would establish our new territories, claiming some bars for our own and conceding others. The thought so depressed me that again I almost turned around.

But anger propelled me. I could sit in public, alone and composed, for one drink.

This bar, despite being tucked into the corner of a pricey restaurant, enjoyed its own identity: a small, dim, intimate place, full of polished brass and gleaming wood, a place where a woman could have a drink alone without feeling conspicuous. Behind the bar reigned smiling Lila.

With an abundance of long blond curls spiraling down her back, Lila looked, from behind, like a teenager. When she turned to face newcomers, her pretty, heavily made-up face, stamped by decades of late nights tending bar, must have surprised them.

She excelled at making people feel like she was happy they'd walked in, like she'd been waiting. Her timing was impeccable. She knew when to offer another pour, when to busy herself so as not to intrude, and when patrons needed her to lean in for some chat. Her most devoted regulars, divorced and widowed older men, vied for a spot at the bar and for her attention.

That night, after performing a quick scan of the place, I grabbed the last open spot at the end and ordered a glass of wine.

Lila clinked it down in front of me. "Nice to see you, sweetie." In anyone else, her habit of calling everyone "sweetie" would have grated me. I leaned back, took a sip, and took a breath.

But something was wrong. Only a few minutes before, the possibility of an encounter with Dutch or mutual friends had nauseated and terrified me. Now that the most desirable possible outcome had been achieved, the coast clear, I felt freshly crushed.

Suddenly, my presence did not feel like the beginning of my crawl back to myself. It did not feel like an act of courage. It felt like a slip, as if I had inadvertently made the most terrible choice and become the focal point in a grim snapshot, a woman alone at a bar. Only now I was even more tragic than at home, because now, my tragedy was on display.

While estranged from Johnny Cash in *Walk the Line*, June Carter played an autoharp before a darkened crowd. She sang about what she'd been promised, about being left, a neglected flower. She sat alone on the stage, her pain spot-lit and exposed.

Why had I not come with my friends, who would have been encouraged by this sign of life? Why had I come at all? *Too late now.* I resolved to finish my wine.

In a brief lull when all the patrons were engaged in their own conversations, their glasses full, Lila joined me at the end of the bar. "I've been wondering about you. I haven't seen you around."

"I've been lying low."

Lila nodded, full of sympathy. "I heard about you and Dutch. I'm so sorry it didn't work out."

The sound of his name sucked the breath out of me.

Lila was still nodding. "He came in with a friend from out of town." Her snapping fingers, as she tried to remember, sounded like rain on a window. "Jimmy." I shuddered. "You probably know Jimmy."

Dutch has been here. He's been going out.

"Anyway, Dutch told me what happened."

He told her what happened. A bartender, in passing.

I stared at Lila, who continued. "He said the nicest things about you. Said he wished you all the best."

He wishes me all the best.

I had predicted that interminable nighttime would ultimately level me. But it wasn't that, or my parents and friends telling me they'd never liked Dutch anyway, or the week I was supposed to join him and his family in Memphis, which I instead passed alone in the echo chamber of my apartment, or my hunt through my desk for a spare phone charger, which instead led me to the red envelopes and cream stationery that I would never use again.

It was this that finally did it, a friendly acquaintance trying to help by relaying his *best wishes.*

I was still staring at Lila, then down at her hand, resting on my forearm. I dug into my purse for my wallet and, finding only a twenty, dropped it on the bar next to my full glass of wine. Then I walked out without a word, leaving Lila standing there, her face flickering with confusion.

I walked without seeing. *Look at my girlfriend.* The pink dress still hung in my closet. I would burn it.

Or.

My blurry gaze fell on my ring, sparkling on my finger, mocking me. I would throw this giant lie in the snow, in the woods.

Lurching toward the creek, the idea made me laugh out loud, a dry, ugly bark. Yes. I would throw it. Why not feed all my sapphires to the snow? Why even try to keep anything beautiful in my possession? Wrenching it from my finger, hurling it with all my force, watching the whiteness swallow it: in this I'd find some small, acrid scrap of poetry.

Beside the creek, I paused. In the stillness of the woods, the ring winked at me.

I couldn't throw it. I couldn't even tuck it away in some drawer, out of sight. And here again came the same tide that had held me all these months. The anger ebbed, and in rushed the aching, the aching.

I pictured us in these woods together as I'd told him the story of Nan's ring. How he had looked at me as he listened, snow clinging to his eyelashes, how his face had shone with love, how sure I'd been then of the central place I occupied in his full, nourishing light. I pictured the house with the pink garden, occupied by others. I pictured us at the cottage, which I would never see again. He would bring other women there now, maybe already had.

The image of the cottage standing alone, empty, hurt worse. In my mind I saw it on the bluff, its dark windows gazing out onto the lake, holding the ghost of Dutch and me together.

I wished that on those trips I had realized that they would one day end. I hadn't considered the possibility and so had been careless with my storage of the details: what exactly we had talked and laughed about, how the water had looked, how our skin had felt pressed together, sun-warmed and slick with sunscreen. With enough time, I knew, some of these details would fade like printed pages, disintegrate, and be lost.

I also knew, standing in the enveloping darkness of the woods, that one detail would remain with me. Dutch had told me I couldn't follow him to the sandbars. I had tried and failed. And when he lifted me off the sand and I looked in his eyes, I swore I had seen triumph there.

8

Three years later, Fiona married Denny in the church that her family had belonged to for decades. Denny was by all accounts kind and steady, just the sort of man we all pictured for her. They delayed their inevitable union only because they had first wanted to save for a bigger down payment on a house, just the sort of responsible decision we all expected of them, and they intended to immediately fill that house with kids. Their engagement announcement was met with a happy chorus of "It's about time."

Before the ceremony, an assortment of Fiona's female relatives and the other bridesmaids and I gathered around her in a dressing room at the back of the church. We hovered and fussed to a steady soundtrack of "shit" and "fuck," a common and perfectly acceptable practice in many Irish circles, sprinkled into conversation for emphasis. Even Fiona's prim great-aunt, seated in a wingback chair in the corner, muttered obscenities as she frowned and rubbed at a spot on her dress.

Claire and I took turns fumbling with seemingly thousands of tiny, uncooperative, satin-covered buttons running the length of Fiona's back. Claire struggled, her jaw clenched and her frustration mounting, until she finally barked, "Jesus Christ!"

An appalled hush fell over the room.

Claire flushed. "I'm so sorry," she murmured. "I shouldn't have said that."

Finished at last, we gathered around Fiona, admiring her. In her modest ivory gown and her mother's lace veil, she looked just as lovely as we all knew she would.

Walking down the center aisle toward the altar, I took in the smiling, expectant congregation and noted how the Irish always found one another. We lived in the same neighborhoods, and the kids attended the same Catholic schools. The seniors volunteered for the Hibernians and the Emerald Society, while the mothers took their daughters to Irish dance classes. The fathers frequented the Gaelic League and coached their sons' teams at Gaelic Park. We all went to the same churches. On and on we overlapped, forming interlocked and homogenous circles, so that at large gatherings like this one, I scanned the sea of faces and recognized almost everyone.

Tim, whose arm I held, was also interconnected. We had first met at the engagement party, and my parents had asked the name of the groomsman with whom I'd been paired. When I told them, my dad nodded. "I went to school with his dad. He was a year ahead of me, but we knew each other." It always went that way.

As we lined up to walk down the aisle, my hem swished dangerously close to my high heels. "I just know I'm going to trip," I whispered to Tim.

"Don't worry," he whispered back. "We got this." Once he had deposited me without incident at the front of the church, he moved into position, flashed me a small smile, and pretended to wipe sweat from his brow. *Whew.*

During the Mass, Fiona and Denny left their post at the front of the church and walked hand in hand to a side altar, where they laid a bouquet at the feet of a large statue of Mary. Watching them, I remembered an observation I had made to my parents as a preteen.

"You know how people always pray to Mary, and hang up pictures of her in their houses and name churches after her and fill the churches up with statues of her?"

Their faces question marks, they had looked at me.

"It's like Mary is God. And not some old guy or Jesus. Not really, even though we say that."

They spent the next hour trying to correct me, and I wished I'd never brought it up. From then on, I always found a subversive pleasure in the idea of Catholics as an army of unwitting feminists, of a woman running the show.

When it was all said and done, the reception underway, the

formalities of cake cutting and toasts and first dances concluded, I watched Fiona and Denny make their rounds. They stopped at each table to greet their guests, some of whom were efficient in their hugs and offers of congratulations. The oblivious ones held the couple hostage, talking at length.

They were nearing James, whom I had glimpsed throughout the day. And if his demeanor was slightly subdued as he chatted and circulated and smiled, I hardly perceived the difference. When Fiona and Denny approached his table, I leaned forward in my seat.

James stood. He hugged Fiona, pecked her on the cheek, and shook Denny's hand. He said something that made them both smile. Then Fiona and Denny greeted the rest of the table and moved on.

Sweet James. I watched him fade into the background of the party. I had never given him enough credit.

I slipped into the ladies' lounge and found Claire, perched on a loveseat, gingerly rubbing her feet.

I eased out of my own heels. "Smoke?"

"Smoke."

Carrying our shoes and clutches and drinks, we padded barefoot out to the stone terrace. Lighting cigarettes, we sank onto a bench facing the banquet room. The candlelit enclosure looked like a giant snow globe, the party within approaching full swing, the crowd milling and starting to dance.

Claire studied them. "Every mick for miles, huh?"

"Of course." I sipped and draped an arm over her shoulders. "I got one for you, Claire. What do you call two single women pushing forty in matching bridesmaid dresses?"

"Assholes." Claire grinned. "They're called assholes. But don't say 'pushing forty.' We're not."

"We're past thirty-five. That's 'pushing.'"

"Well, here's the silver lining. Fiona didn't line us up in front of everyone and make us fight over her bouquet with all the teenagers."

We laughed together.

Claire gestured at the wall of glass before us. “If one more person asks me where my date is or why I don’t have one, you’re going to see a big Claire-shaped hole in that glass.” She sipped her beer. “I got one for *you* now.”

“Hit me.”

“Guess how many people here have said, ‘Hey, Claire. How’s work going?’ Or ‘Hey, Claire. Heard you got promoted, heard you’re management now. Congratulations!’ Just guess.”

I exhaled. “Let me think.”

She sent a plume of smoke curling into the air over her head. “I could be a Supreme Court justice and it wouldn’t matter with this crowd. If you’re a woman and you’re not married and you don’t have kids, you’re a failure.”

“Right. And you know how panicked our parents were when we hit thirty and weren’t married. That was nothing. Imagine the frenzy they’ll work themselves into after this wedding.”

Claire nodded. We sipped and smoked. I thought of my parents, inside at Fiona and Denny’s reception, no doubt admiring and engaging every child in their vicinity.

As a kid, I had always known when I shared space with an adult who hated kids. My mom’s family was full of them, and if they regarded me at all, their displeasure sent me scurrying. But kids also sensed an adult’s predisposition to love them, and my parents were those people. Their immediate and effusive warmth drew kids to them, willing to answer my parents’ questions and accept their pats and praise. My parents seemed destined to be grandparents.

They also seemed like people who would have had a whole slew of kids. “Our own football team,” my dad had said. “We wanted that. We tried.”

But after multiple miscarriages, their doctor had advised them to stop. “He told me I couldn’t keep putting my body through that,” my mom had explained to me once, as if her body were the only collateral damage.

The miscarriages weren’t a secret. I had known about them for most of my life and had occasionally asked questions, prompted by fantasies of phantom brothers and sisters. After a friend of mine had miscarried and been offered a folder bulging with resources, I asked my mom, "Did you ever get any kind of support?"

"That wasn't really an option then," she said. "It wasn't like it is now. It was very common, and when it happened, you just got on with it." The clip of her words suggested stoicism, but her eyes suggested something else.

For years, I'd watched my parents swoon over babies. For years, these encounters had elicited a breathy "We can't wait for your wains." To them, it was only a matter of time.

When they said it, part of me wanted to rail against them. Part of me wanted to laugh, and I felt both impulses under the heft of such a presumption. But they said it with a sighing sincerity that I couldn't bring myself to crush, saying only, "No promises."

I asked Claire, "Do you ever feel lucky to have brothers and sisters?"

"I thought you were the lucky one when we were growing up." Claire lit another cigarette. "You always had new stuff, your own bedroom, privacy."

I'd also had my parents' undivided attention. A kid like Claire, who'd thrown elbows to be seen and get a seat, may have envied me that.

"How about now?" I asked her.

"Do I feel lucky now, you mean?"

"Yeah. I'm the only shot my parents have. But in a family like yours, the parents can spread their expectations around a little. If one kid is a train wreck, they have backups."

"You must be thinking of Kiernan."

"I am, yeah," I admitted.

In addition to four sisters, Claire had one brother. Kiernan was twenty-eight, twice divorced, and a compulsive gambler—not a very good one, judging by the frequency with which he asked to borrow money.

Claire chuckled. "Yeah. He's useless."

"But maybe your parents can console themselves with you and your sisters," I speculated.

"Maybe." Claire considered. "But they're still more interested in my imaginary husband and kids than in my actual life."

"Mine, too." I hitched up my strapless bra. "We're in the same boat."

"No, we're not."

I shielded my eyes and made a show of looking around. "Do you see my husband or kids around here?"

Claire arched an eyebrow. "Everyone can see that you have a very promising *prospect*, though. That means there's hope for you."

She was right. No one had missed Tim's attentiveness at the rehearsal at the church. There, the small, stern woman charged with directing the ceremony had clapped to get everyone's attention. Like obedient children, we all filed into the pews for her lecture, and I ended up sitting in the middle of a crowded pew. Tim, seated at the end, had crawled over everyone in between to get to me, apologizing along the way for the jostled knees and grazed toes. When he landed beside me and started to speak, the church lady cut him off with a bark. "Let's get started."

He sought me out at the rehearsal dinner afterward and offered to drive me home. At the first opportunity, I cornered Fiona, who had coupled us to walk down the aisle together. "Are you matchmaking here, Fi?"

"I'm not. I just paired everyone up based on height. " Fiona gave me an encouraging smile. "Keep an open mind, though. Good guy."

As I chatted with Tim, I felt eyes on us. I pretended not to see the approving smiles and knowing nudges, and I steeled myself when Fiona's mom advanced. "He's single, you know." She lowered her voice, her tone confiding and pointed. "Good guy."

Of course he was. I watched, chuckling, as he allowed the photographer to position him in unnatural, embarrassing poses reminiscent of high-school yearbook photo shoots. While the other groomsmen grimaced and had to be coaxed, Tim cooperated with a smile.

I watched him offer an arm to one of Denny's elderly relatives, who walked with a cane. They chatted as he escorted her to her seat, their pace glacial.

Walking to my car, I watched as he helped Denny load his. Denny was a good guy. Good guys were friends with other good guys.

Even without these commendations, Tim's goodness showed right away, around the eyes. And he was cute, I thought, in a wholesome, outdoorsy way. With his easy smile and dark beard, he would have fit right into a Subaru or LL Bean commercial. But his interest made me uneasy, and when he approached toward the end of the reception, I knew what was coming.

His goodness would have been wasted on me. In a gentle tone, I said, "I'm not dating right now."

I tried, at listless intervals. One of those dates mentioned that he had three sons.

"Really? How old?"

"Five," he told me.

"Wow, triplets."

He shifted in his seat. "No. Not triplets."

Another date took me to an Italian restaurant, where I started with a glass of wine. I raised an eyebrow when he ordered a glass of milk, then again when he requested a pitcher of ranch dressing. When he drowned his lasagna in it, I set down my fork, too revolted to eat my own food.

Ten minutes into a date with a third man, he eyed me with suspicion. "And you're how old?"

I cooled in an instant. "Thirty-six."

"Why haven't you ever been married?"

"That's a complicated question." I glanced at the time on my phone. "Why haven't you?"

"That's different."

"Why is that different?"

"I'm a guy."

He talked at length about a country music festival he'd attended and sulked when I told him I didn't like the genre. He gave a detailed account of his gun collection.

The check had not yet arrived. I was a hostage for at least a few more minutes. *Fuck it.* "What do you need all those guns for?"

"What do you mean?"

"I mean, who do you think is coming?"

He stared at me. "That's not the point."

"What's the point?"

"The point is, it's my right to have them."

His face contorted as if he'd just discovered a hair in his mouthful of food. "Wait. Are you a *liberal*?"

When he texted me for a second date, I laughed out loud.

Other men expressed interest. And just as a baby recoiled from someone she immediately understood was not her mother but a stranger who sounded and smelled and felt all wrong, I jerked away.

I abandoned dating in favor of other endeavors, including church. I delighted my parents when I began joining them for Mass every Sunday for the first time since my teens. They had long hoped for my return to the fold.

"And," my mom said in a hushed tone as we entered, "maybe you'll meet someone nice."

"I'm not here to troll men," I whispered, sliding into the pew. Then I glanced around the church, looking for men. Seeing only smiling old people and families, I settled back and pondered the massive crucifix suspended above the altar.

I'd once heard a fiery homily about the importance of crucifix imagery. A simple bare cross on your neck, or hanging in your home, didn't suffice, the priest had stormed. The crucifix, in all its graphic gore, served as a necessary reminder of what Jesus had endured for us.

When I later relayed this to my Lutheran friend Jenna, she had shaken her head. "See, that would never happen in my church. We're like Diet Christians. We don't need a lot of Jesus and guilt and fanfare, just a nice, watery version."

After my first return to church, I met Fiona and Claire for lunch. "They changed the words to the Mass," I sputtered, once we sat down. "They never change *anything*, and suddenly, the words we've been saying our whole lives are different. Did you know that?"

I looked first at Fiona, who of course knew that. She volunteered, "It's because—"

"It's because they want us to look like dicks," Claire said darkly. "They want the heathens who don't go to Mass all the time to stand out."

"That's exactly how it felt." Sitting in the pew beside my parents, suddenly saying all the wrong words, my past shoddy attendance shone beneath a giant spotlight.

Still, the old people and families greeted me when I sat down among them. They smiled and pumped my hand. They lifted their voices in earnest for hymns and prayers and exuded a peace that awed me.

For a while, I enjoyed pretending I made sense there. But even though I showed up and listened and tried, I could not find what others seemed to. This sense of failing and being eluded had followed me from childhood, when my squirming presence in the pew was mandatory, and as an adult in church, I felt no more connected to God than I did in the DMV. Then I ran into Noelle.

Noelle was one of Glick's many ex-girlfriends, a woman I still crossed paths with in town. When Glick and Noelle first got together, he had brought Dutch and me to Noelle's apartment one night, explaining on the way that she taught yoga. "Limber," he'd added. "Know what I'm saying?"

"We get it, Glick."

When we'd arrived, we found Noelle waving a stick of sage in the air and burning different candles for different specific intentions. Later that night, she'd told me about my aura.

When I bumped into her in the grocery store, she said, "You should try my class. It's very meditative, very healing." She said, "Yoga quiets the mind."

My mind ran in futile circles. I signed up.

Claire rolled her eyes when I told her. "Enough with the yoga, already."

"I think it's a great idea," Fiona said.

When I arrived at the studio, I made two horrifying discoveries. One was the floor-to-ceiling mirrors on every wall. I hadn't realized that students were meant to study their reflections from every angle. The other was that every single student looked exactly like Noelle, the room a field of long, taut, willowy reeds wearing only sports bras and tiny briefs. They draped across their mats, stretching and preening, supremely athletic, utterly fatless.

I unrolled my mat and took my place among them, looking and feeling hopelessly lumpy and malformed, unable to escape the comparison. The mirror was the only place to look.

Noelle entered and arranged herself at the front of the room, poised to begin. Before she could, I scrambled to my feet and practically tackled her, whispering, "I have diarrhea. I'll be back."

Understanding, serene, Noelle nodded. I bolted from the room and never returned, leaving my mat behind.

I made a series of phone calls to therapists, partially covered by my shoddy insurance. One called me back, a wan, unsmiling man who took copious notes and said little.

Each session he began by asking, "How are you doing?"

Unsure where to start, I rambled and shifted in the modern, uncomfortably low-backed chair. After about fifteen minutes, when I'd run out of things to say, he crossed his legs and folded his hands in his lap. "Now, why don't you tell me how you're really doing?"

Each time, I paid a fifty-dollar co-pay on my way out. Each time, I drove home fuzzier than when I arrived. At our eighth session, I broke up with him, stammering, "I'm not sure this is what I want."

"What is it that you want?"

I wanted my four hundred dollars back.

Fiona said, "You can find a new therapist."

"Or you can just drink more," Claire offered, joking. I considered what alcohol did for other people, how it washed away feeling, drowning it. The idea of feeling nothing had once repelled me, but now, I circled it, drawn.

I thought I couldn't feel worse than I did. But rather than drowning my grief, alcohol amplified it, forcing a slideshow of images clicking past.

Click. Dutch pulling from the oven a dinner he'd labored over and, a second later, dropping it on the kitchen floor. We fell beside the spectacular mess and roared with helpless laughter.

Click. Dutch looking at me the night I wore the pink dress, looking at me like he'd never need to look at anyone else again.

Click. His house, or what used to be. It sat on a main artery of our town, and driving past it after we broke up, I saw a FOR SALE sign in front of it. After it sold, I sometimes spotted a middle-aged couple sitting on the porch.

My orange toothbrush sat in a cup on your bathroom counter. I wanted to pull over and explain it to the couple. Some women brought personal items to their partners' homes, cautiously planting them like little flags to see if they would stick. But Dutch bought the toothbrush for me.

My coffee pot took up a corner of your kitchen counter. This was also his idea and his purchase. He didn't drink coffee. He said he just hated how, when we woke up in the morning, I always left to go buy some.

Your bedroom. Dutch's bed, the blue-gray cotton sheets, cool and soft when we climbed in, soon warm and damp and imprinted. We broke the frame.

Your living room. Dutch's couch, the blanket on it, the weight of it wound around us. His house, our cocoon. His house, now inhabited by strangers.

I struggled to stop the images. The more I struggled, the faster and more insistently they came.

Click. Lying knotted in bed, talking about going to the cottage the next morning. Tossing and turning, too giddy to sleep. Facing each other, the alarm clock glowing blue: three a.m. "We could go now." Springing out of bed, throwing our bags in the car, barreling through the darkness toward the lake, fingers entwined across the console. *Click, click, click, click.*

The more I drank, the more the shore receded from view. *Where are you, Dutch?*

The shore disappeared altogether. I abandoned my experiment.

He was lost to me. I was lost to me. In the mirror, I saw a jumble of fragments resembling a person, and didn't know her at all.

9

I realized one night that the man sitting next to me at the bar was an old crush from high school. Back then, I'd swooned over his muscle car, his flat cap that made him look like he worked on the Dublin docks, his long wallet chain. I'd positioned myself front and center at his punk band's shows.

A wallet chain still swung at his leg. Now, in our mid-thirties, it looked ridiculous.

In every other way, he was indistinguishable from the solitary, defeated men lining the bar, hunched over their drinks, saturating themselves before facing whatever waited at home or another day on jobs they hated. I wanted to ask him what had happened.

After a few minutes of uninspired chat, he bought me a Budweiser. As I drank it, he looked me up and down and told me I should go home with him.

I snorted into my beer. "Come on."

"Come on," he wheedled. "You don't have anywhere else to go."

"What makes you say that?"

"You wouldn't be here by yourself if you did."

I took a swig, thinking. "When was the last time you took a woman on a date?"

"You want to go on a date?"

"No. I don't want to go on a date. I'm just curious when you last did that. If ever."

He smirked a little as he polished off his drink.

"Because that's a thing," I continued. "An actual thing some men do. They don't just throw a beer at a woman and call it good. They try a little."

He shrugged.

"You didn't know? It's true." I swiveled toward him on my

stool. It felt so good, for once, not to be the bowl. "Your dad never taught you this? Any fucking manners?"

He shrugged again, unoffended. "I don't know what you want me to say. But you'll get off if you go home with me."

"So I did," I told Claire and Fiona later.

Fiona looked baffled. "You did what?"

"Go home with him."

"How was it?" Claire asked.

"Hard. And then, over. No pretense of exchanging numbers or getting together again. I don't think we even said goodbye when I left."

Fiona looked dubious. "He sounds like an ass."

"He was. That's why it worked."

I'd found my next phase.

They weren't all bad men, which were so easy to find, which, like good men, showed everything one needed to know around the eyes. Some of them made up a different, more problematic category, men currently embattled in or fresh off a divorce. Having lost spouses, homes, children, dogs, money, and their entire understanding of how their lives made sense, they shared a shattered look that I learned to recognize.

Sometimes, they wanted only to fuck their way through their divorces and appreciated a tidy opportunity. But this fragile, unpredictable group sometimes wanted to talk about what they'd lost or what had been taken from them. They described their ex-wives as devils who'd ruined them or angels they'd taken for granted, sometimes both. Their accounts were venomous or anguished, sometimes both.

Some of these men also wondered, after the sex, when their lives came rushing back to them, if perhaps I might be the solution to their crises. Doug, a web designer divorced by someone named Lisa, was one of them.

At his apartment, Doug's cat Smoky sat beside us as we had sex. Its relentless mewing unnerved me, and I wished Doug would push it off the bed. When I climbed on top, the cat swiped at my ankle, drawing blood. I yelped and scrambled away. "Aw." Doug sat up and rubbed the cat's head. "Smoky's playing with you."

Afterward, as I hunted through the bedding and on the floor for my clothes, he talked about the upcoming destination wedding of a co-worker, a mutual friend of his and Lisa's. He wondered aloud if Lisa would go. He wondered if Lisa would bring a date. He wondered, suddenly, if he should bring me as his date. Maybe seeing him with someone else would make Lisa finally realize her mistake and what a bitch she'd been.

"What do you think? I'll pay for airfare and the hotel."

I declined.

Some of my friends judged me. Some envied me. I heard both in James' exclamation, "You're fucking around like a *guy*."

"She can do what she wants," Fiona barked. "*You* do. She's having fun."

I didn't consider this fumbling in the dark fun. It simply gave me what alcohol had not, what Dutch had described when he told me about taking pills. It allowed me to feel nothing.

The desire for this kind of reprieve made me like the divorced men. And after the sex, I returned to my life and tried to occupy it in a way that looked normal.

I taught and attended endless meetings. I filled my free time with family and friends. I moved to a nicer apartment with a small balcony where I placed a lounge chair for reading, built-in shelves I filled with books, and a broken fireplace I filled with candles.

All the while I seemed to be moving forward with the business of life, and I was, in a sense. But I was also waiting, always waiting, for Dutch.

Throughout our thirties, he reappeared again and again. After months of silence, I'd hear my phone chime and look down to find a message from him, always initiating some careless conversation as if we had just spoken the day before. My hands shook as I read the texts.

Sometimes they came in a flurry and stopped as abruptly as

they had begun. Sometimes they culminated in a phone conversation that lasted several hours, like the one he initiated on my thirty-eighth birthday. He called again on my thirty-ninth. On my fortieth, I expected the call and cut short my night with friends in anticipation. When my phone still had not rung at one a.m., I climbed into bed, hollow.

He disappeared again and again. I relearned to lose him each time. But no matter how much time passed, no matter what was happening in my life, I responded when he contacted me. I would not stop myself. Something inside me that quieted in his absence ignited when he resurfaced.

"Block him," Claire told me. "Or change your number."

"I can't."

"What do you mean? Why not?"

I managed a weak smile. "Because then he won't be able to contact me."

Each time he resurfaced, the memories of suffering flew away all at once, like birds. Only the good remained, only the warmth of the light, only the joy when I heard that deep, rumbling, laughing voice.

I examined our pattern again and again and every time threw it to the side in helpless frustration. He came and went. He'd always come and gone. He would always come and go. These were the verb tenses of Dutch. But whether his coming or his going meant more, I could not see. Whether I was too important to abandon or too easy to discard, I could not see. I could not understand the truth of us.

When Fiona and Denny had their son, Liam, they invited their family and friends, including Tim and me, to the baptism. They did it again two years later after their daughter Maggie's birth. They hosted backyard barbeques and holiday parties and Super Bowl parties, doing what people with kids did, skipping the hassle of finding a sitter and instead bringing their friends to them. Every time I saw Tim at these gatherings, he smiled and approached.

He always asked, "Still not dating?"

"Still not dating."

In the meantime, I slowly faced the fact that I dreaded my job, which, in earning my Master's, I had gone to great trouble and into great debt to procure. I'd spent the sum of myself on one man and come up empty, and I wondered if I'd duplicated this mistake with my career.

Every semester, a small handful of students made me want to keep trying. They were so earnest, so awake, so worthy of a good teacher. They deserved something useful to take with them.

But so many others spent class huddled inside their hoodies, inexplicably, perpetually chilly and physically compromised, their eyes dull. Lacking the decency to sit in the back, they slept or texted through my lectures from the front row. Their attendance was spotty, and when they did show up, the activity of the classroom so befuddled them that they might as well have stayed home.

Why then, I thought, did I spend hours preparing lesson plans? Why did I spend entire weekends poring over papers they had written the night before? The ones not blatantly plagiarized were largely incoherent. And why did I even bother wading through the tedium of research and citation methods, which the Department Chair said must be taught? They lived online, I reasoned. They could figure it out for themselves.

The Chair liked my recent publication of an essay on Virginia Woolf. He asked me, as a new semester approached, to stop by his office.

"Would you like to teach a section of Women's Lit?"

The offer flattered and terrified me. In the right hands, courses like this could be a life raft for anyone actually listening, as I had been in college.

Still, the responsibility felt weighty and perilous. *I can't possibly be the right person for this.*

As if reading my mind, he said, "You're more than qualified. This is an opportunity to diversify your teaching experience."

He told me I could create my own syllabus. He told me I

could choose the readings and projects. I shifted in my seat, picturing it. A few students would want to be there. Many more would register because their schedules and graduation requirements accommodated no alternative.

The Chair folded his hands on his desk. "You'll have a great deal of freedom with a course like this. It can be whatever you want it to be."

I accepted and thanked him. On the first day, I entered the classroom wearing the jeans that made me feel youthful, the heeled boots that made me feel armored, and a smile that hid my trepidation.

I gave what I considered a low-stakes overview: why there was value in and a need for a course like this, why literature by and about and for women mattered, why a feminist perspective must inform such a course.

A hand shot up. "But I'm not a feminist."

No matter how many times I'd heard women say this, it still floored me. "When you say you're not a feminist, what does that mean?"

"Well, I have a boyfriend," the young woman explained.

I steepled my fingers. "Are feminism and boyfriends mutually exclusive?"

The young woman's face went blank.

I asked the group for a show of hands. "Who here identifies as a feminist?"

Four hands rose.

"Okay." I paused. "Let's try this. This might actually be a good starting point. Everyone, take a minute and write down your definition of 'feminist.' Send them up when you're ready."

I read them aloud: *battle axe, angry woman, unattractive woman, man hater*.

I finished reading amid the chuckles and asides. Then I said, "I'm going to make a few statements, and if you agree, put your hand up. Okay?" I waited. "Women have the same dignity as other human beings."

Most hands.

"Women should do what they want with their lives and their bodies."

Most hands.

"Women should be able to walk around in the world without being degraded or assaulted."

Most hands.

I felt a rising in my throat, an opportunity. With exactly the right words, I could give them what I'd been given. I opened my hands and flattened them on the table. "If you agree with those statements, you're a feminist." My smile was so weak. My delivery was all wrong. "Welcome to the club."

A few met my gaze.

Some were already scrolling through their phones, bored. Others eyed me, suddenly wary of me and my suggestion of membership. I had transformed before their very eyes into the repugnant figure they had described on their scraps of paper.

I glided on to projects, papers, due dates.

A teacher like Fiona would have resolved to give them time, cut them slack. *They're only teenagers.*

I was tired of taking responsibility for other people's education. I was tired of trying to convince people, especially other women, that women were worth something. *Let them take responsibility for themselves.*

A teacher like Fiona would have looked out at this sea of apathetic young faces and worked harder.

I wondered what else I should be doing with my time.

I despaired over my predicament and wondered whether my friends were just better at adulthood. The majority had followed neatly plotted courses without aberration, making professional choices that advanced their interests, elevated them within their respective ranks, and provided them financial stability. Alongside their impressive trajectories, the flaccidity of my own depressed me.

"What are your options?" Claire asked as we wrestled her giant new flat screen through her front door.

"I could stay where I am, probably indefinitely." We maneuvered the box around a tight corner. "Or I could quit teaching. I fantasize about it." What alternative I was qualified for, I had no idea, much less an appealing one that would pay my bills.

Once we had hauled the box to an empty patch of living room wall and rested it there, we paused to catch our breath. Claire asked, "Would you ever go for a PhD?"

In particularly demoralized moments, I had considered it, wondering whether the possibility of more opportunity and money and prestige might improve my outlook. "But when I really think about it," I told Claire, "it probably doesn't make sense to dig even deeper into work I don't like and go even deeper into debt to do it."

She nodded. "I get it. I hate my job too."

I looked over at her. "Do you?"

"Yep. But at this point, where am I gonna go?" She sat down on the floor. "Sometimes I come home from my shitty job to my empty place and look around and think, 'This can't be it.'"

I sat beside her. We surveyed her living room together. "Me too."

Shortly after my forty-first birthday, Fiona and Denny hosted a Christmas party. In stark contrast to my silent apartment, cheerful chaos dominated their house. Everyone brought their kids, along with diaper bags, snacks, sippy cups, and assorted distractions to be dispersed throughout the night. The adults drank and laughed and talked. The little kids bounced on the furniture and swatted at their toys like cats. The older ones tore through the house in a sweaty, noisy herd.

When Fiona's daughter, Maggie, tottered toward me and lifted her arms, I hoisted her into my lap. She collapsed into immediate, almost violent sleep, overcome by the activity of the night, even snoring a little. Five minutes later, she jolted awake to the clatter of her colorful plastic blocks, on which some nearby child had encroached. Down and away she scrambled to regain her rightful possession.

I stood and joined Claire and James. We raised our beers out of harm's way each time the herd thundered by on another lap.

"I just realized," James said, looking around, "we're the only people here who aren't married with kids."

Claire chuckled. "You're a little slow on the draw, buddy."

He lifted his bottle. "To the last ones standing."

We clinked bottles and sipped. I excused myself and stepped outside for a cigarette. Looking up at the starry, frigid sky, I thought about Dutch.

Sometimes he had held me to him and whispered, "Can I come inside you? Please. I need to come in you." Maybe only the impulsivity of pleasure had fueled these lapses in judgment. But I had wondered, too, whether some part of him had wanted what I wanted.

Sometimes I had pictured a child with blond hair, like ours. A boy would be tall like Dutch. A girl would have my green eyes. I had pictured us lying in bed, studying the baby blinking and kicking and nestled between us, trying to decipher the origin of every tiny feature.

But Dutch had said, again and again, that he didn't want that. I had filed it away. The night of the Christmas party, it shone before me as I stood on the driveway, sending intermingled plumes of frosty breath and smoke swirling into the night air.

I didn't cry. I was done with all that now. But I decided then that I would not go alone to Fiona and Denny's upcoming New Year's Eve party, in the same boisterous houseful of families. I brought a handsome, dull, harmless guy whose name I could not later recall, figuring his company might be a slight improvement over facing the party by myself.

This time, Tim hung back. When my date and some other men had congregated in the garage to discuss the merits of various cars, I squeezed through the crowded living room to retrieve another beer from the kitchen. Tim passed me on the way.

"Looks like you're finally out of retirement," he said without stopping. His smile was small and sad.

I spent New Year's Day at my parents' house, the three of us following a script well worn by many years of tradition. After a substantial brunch to absorb the previous night's excess, we set about stripping the house of all the Christmas decorations we'd put up together the day after Thanksgiving.

Before going outside to remove Christmas lights, my dad layered up as if going into Arctic battle, his face set with grim determination. My mom always said, "Be careful on the ladder, Dave."

He always responded, "I've been doing this for years, Maura. You don't have to tell me to be careful."

He headed out to the garage as she and I began boxing up wreaths, stockings, garlands, the small porcelain nativity set on the hearth, the miniature Christmas village arranged on the mantel.

When only the Christmas tree remained, and most of the boxes had been dragged back to the basement, my mom looked mournful. "I *hate* taking down the tree. Let's sit for a bit first." We sat side by side on the couch, listening to my dad's heavy footsteps on the roof.

The tree bore the Waterford ornaments she had been collecting for years, their heavy crystal catching the thin, watery January sunlight from the picture window. Mixed in with them were the cardboard, Styrofoam, and construction paper ornaments I had made as a child and, full of pride, presented to my parents. They had lost most of their glitter and glue and almost entirely disintegrated.

I picked one up and examined it. "These hardly look like ornaments anymore."

"Well, I love them," my mom said. And when I thought she was reaching over to pat my leg or arm, she instead took my hand and lifted it to inspect the sapphire blinking there.

Every time she noticed my ring, I froze. Could she tell that it wasn't Nan's? Did she detect some subtle difference between the two rings that I had missed or forgotten? Every time, I felt afresh the radiating guilt of my deceit, the stinging reproach of my carelessness. She said only, "I'm so glad you wear this."

I twisted it on my finger.

"Did Nan ever tell you the story behind this ring?" She paused. "No, she wouldn't have. You were young." She touched my finger. "This was her engagement ring. She was engaged before she met Dad."

"Really?" I had never considered the possibility of Nan living a life separate and veiled from our family's. "What happened?"

"He went away to war. They were supposed to get married when he came back, but he died." She looked at me. "Sad. I think part of her was always waiting for someone who just never came back."

Me too. The ring twinkled like the crystal ornaments on the tree.

"And then after she and Dad got together, she couldn't wear the ring, obviously. That's why it just sat in a box."

I considered this. "Did your brothers and sisters know she was engaged? Did Grandpa know?" Applying a warm title like *Grandpa* to such a cold person felt as clumsy and stiff as it had when I was a child.

"Peggy and Maeve know. But she never told the boys, I don't think. Or Dad." She gazed at the tree. "Some things only other women understand."

We turned our attention to the clatter at the picture window, where my dad now wrestled with the ladder. "Careful, Dave," came my mom's automatic call.

"I *got* it, Maura." We heard more clattering, then, "*Shit.*"

My mom shook her head.

I studied the frost etching the window. "Grandpa kind of scared me."

"Me too," she agreed. "He was mean, to all of us kids but to Mom especially. He put her down all the time. And he did it in front of anyone—us, the rest of the family, anyone. He didn't care. I hated that."

"Do you think she ever wanted to leave?"

"I know she did. But people didn't get divorced then. Especially Catholics with five kids to raise."

I looked again through the window at my dad, now sporting a large coil of lights on his shoulder. After decades of marriage, he still reached for my mom's hand every time they went out in public together. I couldn't imagine him being *mean* to her.

As if reading my mind, my mom continued, "That's why I married your dad. I knew it would be different. He's such a good man."

I nodded. "He is."

I knew my mom had had boyfriends before my dad. I'd heard a couple names, heard bits and pieces of stories, but I had never asked the question I posed next. "Did you ever love a bad man?"

"What a question." She laughed.

"What? Why?"

"You can't love a bad man."

"Sure you can."

"What I mean is, why would you?" She waved the idea away like a fly. "What a waste. Bad men can't love you back. They only love themselves."

I had sometimes accused her of rigidity and oversimplification. Now I wondered if I had simply failed to grasp the obvious.

She gestured out the window at my dad. "A good man can change everything."

She examined my ring again. "Anyway, I'm glad you wear this. It's too pretty to sit in a box." With a reluctant stretch, she stood. "Let's get this tree down."

The next time I went to Fiona's I asked, "What's Tim been up to?"

She unloaded her dishwasher as we chatted. "Work, travel, the usual."

I leaned on her kitchen counter and tried to sound offhand. "Is he seeing anyone?"

"Not anymore. It didn't work out." She stopped. "Why?"

I shrugged.

She turned to me and broke into laughter. "*Now?* The guy's been trailing after you for five *years.*"

I drummed on the counter. She waved a frying pan in her excitement. "Whatever. Better late than never. Do you want me to give him your number?"

"You can try. He probably doesn't even want it anymore."

He called the next day.

10

By my design, our courtship unfolded slowly. We went on a first date. A week later, we went on another one, and two weeks after that, a third. These were chaste outings, dinner only, and afterward he directed me to sit in my warming car as he scraped and brushed snow from it.

He didn't withhold or bombard. He told me that he was a technical consultant and that he was close to his family. On weekends he played football and bar trivia with his friends. He didn't make me feel suspect or broken for never having been married, saying simply that he hadn't either.

He didn't push or intrude. He asked about teaching and my parents and my favorite music. He told me he'd just finished *Cloud Atlas* on a flight and asked what I liked to read, which touched me. The men I'd known never asked me that, or read books themselves. I was grateful that he didn't press for details about past relationships.

Over one of our dinners, he gestured at my hand. "I like your ring."

I hadn't realized my thumb had found my ring finger and was rubbing the band. Having worn the ring for twelve years, it felt like an organic protrusion on my finger, its removal as unthinkable as an amputation, like the band and the skin beneath it had fused.

He said, "You know, I've never seen you without it."

I was surprised he noticed.

"There must be a story there," he encouraged me.

I sipped my water. "My grandmother left it to me."

"Oh." He waited. Then, "You must have really loved her."

I shifted a little in my seat. "I did."

This part, at least, was true.

Other conversations flowed more easily. We chatted about

our many common friends and acquaintances, movies we both liked, places we'd traveled to or hoped to one day. When he told me his job sent him to a different city each week, Monday through Friday, I nodded. "That's interesting."

"It can be. I definitely thought it would be when I got started." He swallowed a bite. "I guess I didn't realize how much I'd actually just be sitting in a hotel room by myself. It gets boring, and lonely. So it'd be nice to go somewhere *with* someone for a change."

"Well, if you ever want a travel partner, I'm game."

I was being glib. But suddenly, he smiled in a way that made me flush and change the subject.

"I don't know," Claire said after the first date. "I can't really see it."

"Why not?" Fiona was indignant. "He has a degree, nice family, good job… He's perfect."

"He's good on paper," Claire granted. She looked at me. "But you like a Johnny Cash, and Tim is more of a—"

"Donny Osmond?" I offered.

"Yes." She snapped her fingers. "Exactly."

"We only want a Johnny Cash when we're young." Fiona explained it to Claire like a patient teacher. "We outgrow that."

Claire chortled. "Do we?"

"Yes." Fiona was firm. "At a certain point, we're done with train wrecks and ready for a grown-up." She smiled at me. "Right?"

"Let me get to know him before you marry us off, Fi."

After several dates, she asked, "So, would you call him your boyfriend?"

"I think I'm too old to call anyone my boyfriend."

"But you're a couple," she prompted.

"No. We're just seeing each other. That's different."

She and Claire looked at me.

"What's the difference?" Claire asked.

"The difference is that we can see other people."

Fiona always knitted her eyebrows when perplexed. "But you're not seeing other people. And he's not."

"Yeah, but we can if we want to. It's casual."

Claire looked doubtful. "Does he know that?"

"Of course." Seeing that they expected further explanation, I added, "Plus, you know, he's gone all the time."

Tim himself cited this as the biggest obstacle he'd encountered in relationships. "The women I've dated had a hard time with all the traveling," he told me over coffee. After two months, our conversations were expanding. "I guess they thought at first it would be okay, but they got tired of it pretty quickly. They wanted someone who was around more."

I found his regular absences a major selling point. They calibrated the relationship and allowed me to breathe. And because they were dictated by his circumstances and not mine, I didn't have to feel responsible.

When we spent time together on weekends, he was fun and warm and I made him happy by simply showing up. I marveled at how little he needed.

Sometimes when he called and texted during the week, I engaged. Sometimes I wanted to. If I didn't, I said afterward that I had fallen asleep early or forgotten I had silenced my phone.

Sometimes when he asked for more of my time on the weekends—not just a dinner but a whole day, or night, or two—I said yes. Sometimes I wanted to. If I didn't, I said I had plans with friends, papers to grade, family obligations. He never sulked or pushed.

At restaurants he drank beer, but only one or two. He treated servers well. He gradually told me more about himself, and none of these disclosures gave me pause. *This is what an intact person looks like.* Only when I saw his house did I hear a faint alarm.

The first time he invited me over, I pulled up in front of the large colonial and panicked. *He lives with his parents.*

He let me in and poured me a glass of wine. "Dinner's going to be a few minutes. Want a tour?"

I trailed after him, braced for an encounter.

No one else was there. Couch, coffee table, and TV adorned the living room. A soccer ball and overturned bike, balanced on its seat in the midst of a repair, rested in one corner. One of the four bedrooms held a bed and dresser. A mahogany table for eight filled the dining room, its fussily carved legs and matching chairs suggestive of a much older person's taste, perhaps a hand-me-down from an elderly relative.

The rest of the house was resoundingly empty. As I walked through it, my footsteps echoing down the halls and on the staircase, I felt the house waiting, waiting for its occupants, waiting for a life.

On the wall in the cavernous garage, neatly mounted, hung three more bikes, two of them child-sized. I gestured at them questioningly.

"My buddy and his family got rid of a lot of stuff when they moved out of state, so I bought them," he explained. "Figured I might need them down the road."

At dinner, I couldn't refrain from commenting. "This is a lot of house for one person."

"I know. And I'm never here. And it's practically empty, as you can see." He smiled. "When people come over, they always ask if I just moved in, and they're always surprised when I tell them I've been here for years."

Years. I let the word marinate. "What made you decide on this one?"

"Family."

I raised an eyebrow. "Should we be expecting them soon?"

He laughed. "No. I just meant, when I was looking for a house, I knew I'd need some space one day. For family, my own family." His certitude reminded me immediately of my parents'.

Years. He had owned the house for years. It had nothing to do with me. And still I wondered whether maybe it did have something to do with me.

❧

A few months in, he started asking cautious questions about my views on family. The first time he brought it up, I said, "I'm open."

Heartened, he nodded. "What does that mean?"

"It means, family may or may not be in the cards." I spoke with care. "I'm forty-one, and I haven't found the right…circumstances. So I try not to think about it too much."

"Let's say you found yourself in the best possible circumstances, whatever that looks like." He spoke with equal care. "Do you think then you might want kids?"

"Probably. In the best possible circumstances."

"Do you ever wonder, though, if you should think about it more? If maybe you can create those circumstances?" At my swift "no," he ventured a nervous smile. "I guess I think that improves my odds. I think it's proactive."

"I think it's dangerous."

He looked surprised. "Dangerous how?"

"Well, with your career, you can make a plan, set goals, take specific steps. Right? But that doesn't work when it comes to love and family. You can't will love and family into existence."

Fiona was one friend, I told him, whose hopes and realities ultimately aligned. "But I had plenty more, when we were young and single and had no idea what the future really held, who thought they knew."

"What did they think they knew?"

"They thought marriage and parenthood were fixed points on their course."

"And what happened to them?"

"They were wrong." I shrugged. "You could be wrong."

He waited. I settled on a hypothetical. "Let's say you find the perfect girl."

"Let's say I do."

"So you get married. But she's not the perfect girl, she's not who you thought at all. And you end up divorced and sitting in some bar, telling a stranger about it." He tilted his head. "Or you find the perfect girl, but she doesn't want to get married. Or have kids. Ever."

"The perfect girl for me will want to get married and have kids, though," he said, his tone mild. "That's part of my perfect."

"Okay. You meet your perfect girl, and she wants to get married and have kids. Let's say she's adorable, Catholic, a really wholesome PTA type who loves to cook but is also great in bed. The whole nine."

He laughed. "Let's go with this."

"But what if she can't have kids? What if you can't?"

He considered.

"Let's say"—I hesitated—"you find the one you want. And the one you want just doesn't want you back."

He sat quiet, thinking.

I shrugged again to show my remove from these hypotheticals, my lack of investment. "I don't know. But for a lot of people, whatever their vision was, it didn't materialize. They couldn't control it." I wondered if I was hurting him. I didn't want to hurt him. "So I guess," I concluded, "I'm an 'everything possible, nothing guaranteed' kind of gal."

Tim nodded. "I get it. I understand." He paused. "Can I offer an opinion?"

"Sure."

"It sounds like you don't want to be disappointed. That makes sense. And I think it's okay to manage expectations, as long as you still *have* them."

"And *I* think," I said, ready to cap the conversation, "it's okay to have expectations, as long as you still manage them."

"Absolutely," he said.

A single person with that house and four bikes didn't strike me as someone who was managing expectations.

The next time he made me dinner, I started laughing in the middle of it. The dining room table where we sat was so absurdly vast and empty that I couldn't stop myself. When I apologized and explained, he laughed with me, saying, "I know. You should see when it's just me here. It's like a morgue."

He was so good-natured. I was so relieved that I hadn't hurt him. We carried our plates to the living room, the moment warm and agreeable, and settled on the couch in front of the TV.

As we ate and chatted during commercials, he looked around. "I really do think I should liven this place up. I don't know what do with it, though." He glanced over at me as I chewed. "What do you think it needs?"

The last time I'd found myself having this conversation with a man, I'd stood in the full strength of the sun. This time, a shudder passed through me. "Not for me to say," I responded.

Before he could say more, I brought up Fiona and Denny, who planned to meet us at the bar later that night. I ate faster, suggesting we hurry a bit so as not to be late, suggesting it might actually be fun to go early, volunteering to do the dishes. From that night on, when he tried to steer us to his house, I tried to steer us away.

In the spring, we canoed and hiked through the local state park and took long, ambling bike rides. We went to the movies and to dinner. After one night out, as we stood in the parking lot kissing, a flitting, laughing, self-conscious goodbye, he said, suddenly remembering, "Hang on a second."

From his car he drew a copy of the academic journal containing my Virginia Woolf essay. I recognized the marbled maroon cover and flushed with surprise. "Where did you get that?"

"I ordered it. You told me about it. Took a while to show up, but I read it as soon as it came." He grinned. "I have to confess, I had to look up a few things along the way."

I laughed.

He returned the journal to his car. "I'm no scholar, but I thought it was amazing. Congratulations."

"Thank you," I faltered.

He shoved his hands in his pockets. "I just wanted to read it."

No one outside my discipline would have ever heard of this obscure publication, and most people would have found its contents as palatable as a mouthful of sand. That he had tracked it down and waded through it moved me. That he had paid such careful attention to what I said awed me. I had only mentioned it once, in passing. "Thank you."

A voice inside told me to go home. The distance I had maintained the last few months served some vague but important purpose. Instead, I bent to an impulse and kissed him again, my mouth on his more insistent this time, my hands guiding his. Thirty minutes later, he slid into my bed for the first time.

He unwrapped me like a present. He shook like a virgin. He ran his fingers over me as if I were a sculpture, at one point murmuring, almost to himself, "I knew you'd have nice shoulders." He kissed me and kissed me.

In the end, when he cried out and lay shuddering beside me, I felt my carelessness, the weight of it sitting on my chest.

I still said no more than I said yes, trying to measure my presence against my absence. He deferred to me with amiable consistency.

"How's the sex?" Claire asked. "I bet it's really polite, lots of pleases and thank yous. Does he put his jacket on the floor for you to step on before you get into bed?"

I tried to smile along with her. "Not exactly. I think he's attractive. And he makes me feel attractive." His adoration was almost tangible, no matter how much or little energy I mustered during sex, no matter how much or little effort I put into my appearance. With Tim, I stood on the beach, on solid ground, no sandbars in the distance.

"But?"

"I don't know. Sometimes it feels like a little much." The

weight on my chest felt heavier every time we had sex. "Sometimes I shut him down."

Claire chuckled. "The blushing maid."

"That's me."

On occasion, I detected the subtlest note of disappointment in Tim's voice. It evaporated in an instant, and we glided on. He was remarkably accepting. Still, worry gnawed at me. I wondered if his true gift was not acceptance, but extraordinary patience. One looked so much like the other.

I knew it well. I performed it all the time.

11

S*ince dating, Dutch and I have maintained platonic contact. We communicate regularly, and I find great value in our ongoing friendship.*

After Dutch and I broke up, I could hardly bear the general knowledge of our separate coexistence. Specific knowledge of how his life had continued would have annihilated me.

I believed, after our breakup, that he could never represent anything but the blackest hole in my history. That he and I would never achieve anything resembling friendship. That we would never, ever arrive at a point when we told each other about our relationships with other people. And yet, after enough conversations stretching through our thirties and into our forties, we had those conversations,. a wild implausibility that astounded me.

After the silences, our questions about the other's current life cascaded one over another. He wanted details. So did I. We struggled to understand the content of the other's time in our absence. *Are you seeing anyone?* I thought to ask, but I couldn't face the answer and instead said, "Tell me what's new with you."

He'd just bought another house to flip, he said, his sixth to date. His bank account continued to balloon.

Realizing I'd never asked before, I asked then. "What made you sell your first house?" Our cocoon. No matter how many years passed, driving past it still elicited the dull thud of grief.

"After everything with you and me, I couldn't stay." He cleared his throat. "Too sad."

His admission, despite the dousing, revealed an ember still aglow. The house had become haunted for him too.

Do you still see Jimmy? I thought to ask, but I couldn't face the answer and instead asked, "Who do you hang out with these days?"

All the guys from Hurley's, he said, all the usual suspects. When he asked me if I was dating, I told him about Tim.

"It's casual," I said. "He's a good guy."

"Is he an academic?" In his question I detected the faintest tremor.

"No. But he's educated, and he's a reader. Hard to find." I wanted it to sting.

Finally, I felt that I *must* know about his dating life, that if I could face what lurked behind this door like I had all the others, I could face anything. I didn't expect the relief that flooded through me once I cracked it open.

He told me laughingly about his girlfriends, aspiring influencers whose first names sounded like last names, who spent most of their time grooming themselves and posting on social media, who were always beautiful and always much younger. He'd never heard of the music and movies and shows they liked. I listened and rolled my eyes and interjected when my exasperation became too much.

"I keep hearing these news stories of Instagram models that plummet to their deaths trying to get the perfect selfie on the edge of some cliff," I told him. "Why do I feel like you dated the last four?"

"Five," he hooted. "The last five."

"And this is what you're about now, huh?"

"That's what I keep telling myself. But maybe what I really want is someone I can talk to who understands me."

"Maybe."

He faked a heavy sigh. "I think I'm one of those late bloomers who has to take a few laps before he figures it out. Like when I'm sixty. And my girlfriend wants me to take her to get a belly-button ring."

"Because her parents won't sign the consent form."

We chuckled together. During these exchanges, despite the space that stretched between us, I fell back in step beside my best friend. *Oh. It's you.*

His romantic life was a punchline even to him. He tired of

these girls quickly, and I relished his need to find me again and again. Sometimes I even felt something resembling compassion when I thought of the girls he dated. Like me, they must not have known what hit them.

And so we established a new way of being, on the phone. He lamented, but not really. He made the jokes, and I was in on them. The tone of these conversations was so jocular that he could not possibly have imagined that I waited for my boyfriend to leave town at the start of each week. He could not possibly have imagined that once Tim left, I lay on my bed and slid my hands into my panties and closed my eyes.

Dutch hovered there above me, his weight on me, his face close to mine. The moving hands were not my own but his, the commands softly issued. The words were his, and my responses came in whispered rushes. "Tell me you love me."

"I love you."

"Tell me I own you."

"You own me."

"Is there anyone else?"

"There's no one else."

The words were still as true as they had been when I'd first said them, in a dim stairwell at twenty-nine.

When the waves of pleasure receded, he was gone. I was alone in my bed, with wet eyes and wet hands, pathetic and tragic and grotesque.

One night, after not speaking for a few months, Dutch called me. Hearing the giddiness in his voice, my stomach churned. After abbreviated banter, he told me he'd met someone special. They were getting married.

"You're getting married?" Suddenly, we seemed to be speaking through tin cans, connected by a string pulled taut.

"I'm getting married!" he repeated. They were scrambling to plan a fast wedding and buy a house. So much to do before the baby arrived.

"She's pregnant?" I sank onto my couch, clutching my phone.

They were already talking about getting married when they got the news, he told me. He loved her. The pregnancy just expedited a marriage that would have happened anyway.

"And you love her."

"I love her deeply."

He went on for a few more minutes, and I stupidly echoed what he said. No words of my own would come. At the end of the conversation, I said a final time, my voice dull and flat, "And you love her."

"I love her deeply."

When the call ended, I remained on my couch for a long time. I held my phone in my lap like a paperweight and rolled the woman's name around in my mouth like a marble. I rotated the sapphire on my finger.

I would have thought a moment like this would resemble a movie, thunderous and spectacular and full of fanfare. But I was still. My apartment was still. Quiet settled over it.

The following day, I asked Fiona to meet me. It had to be Fiona, who would still listen to the story she'd been listening to for years, who would refrain from issuing all the obvious indictments, whose patience proved boundless. We met at the bar that night.

When I had explained it all, every gruesome detail, she squeezed my hand. "I can't believe she's pregnant."

"I know," I said miserably. "He said he *never* wanted kids. And he's never lived with anyone before. And now they're buying a *house* together. Some goddamn mansion, I guess."

"Did he tell you anything else?" Fiona asked.

"She sounds so *normal*. She's not some Amber Alert, she's our age. She has a degree, nice family, good job…" I dropped my face into my hands.

"I never knew…" I saw how hard she was trying not to injure me further. "I never knew how it would play out with you guys."

"*I* knew. I was sure that this thing between us was"—I wiped my face—"written. I thought we were too young when we met, and that circumstances would keep us apart, and other people and life and bad timing, and then, you know, one day..." I shook my head. "Then one day, finally, we'd be together. Because I'm his June Carter."

I had believed it. And as I said it out loud, I recognized in Fiona's expression the same pity I had felt for Dutch's girlfriends when he had described them to me.

She went quiet. Then, "What are you going to do about Tim?"

"I'm going to bring him to the wedding."

"Are you *crazy*?" For just a second, Fiona's usual decorum escaped her. "Dutch invited you? Why would he do that?"

I laughed as I rubbed my eyes. "I think because we're such good *friends* now. Army buddies. Maybe we'll high five at the church."

"No." Fiona shook her head. "No, no, no. This will kill you. You can't go to this."

"I have to, Fi." I thought then of the hundreds of hours of murder shows I'd watched after the breakup, how families always said the same thing about their missing. Without a body, they were always waiting for their loved one to walk through the door.

I had also been waiting. But here, after all these years of missing, was the body of my relationship with Dutch. Here was the irrefutable pronunciation of death.

I dropped against the back of my chair. Fiona leaned over to take my hands, and we sat like that, holding hands across the table like sisters.

"Tell me why," she insisted. "Why do you have to?"

Because I'm porcelain that loves a hammer.

Because the ones who break us own us.

I swallowed. "Because I have to see this for myself."

❧

When I opened the door for Tim, he whistled. "You look great. Is that a new dress?"

"It's a really old dress," I told him. "I'm almost ready."

He waited in my living room. I retreated to the bathroom for a final inspection, turning around and around in the full-length mirror. I hadn't thought the pink dress would ever emerge from my closet again.

And now, after all these years, it still fit.

In the midst of the horrors that lay ahead, I would claim one moment. Dutch would see me, and for an instant he would forget the woman in white beside him. He would remember the last time he'd seen me in the pink dress, how he'd felt then, what he'd said. *Look at my girlfriend.* I did a slow, final turn.

Animated by our field trip, Tim chatted throughout the two-hour drive. "So we're going straight to the reception?"

"Yeah, the service would have been a drag." My fantasies about going to the church had included Dutch calling the wedding off when he saw me, Dutch saying my name at the altar, me standing to speak when the minister asked if anyone objected to the union. But this was the stuff of corny sitcoms and movies. The service now concluded, nothing more could be done. I typed the address of the reception into Tim's navigation app.

"And how do you know these people?" he asked.

"I never met her. I know the guy." I swallowed the acid working its way up my throat. "He's an old friend."

"From where?" Tim's eyes flitted between the road and the dashboard.

"Um, from the bar. Back in the day." I looked out the window. "I haven't seen him in ages. I'm surprised he invited me."

He hit the gas and searched for music to match his buoyancy. I gripped the armrest and tried to keep the snake of nausea from uncoiling.

Passing signs for Dutch's hometown was like approaching Oz. *I've always wanted to see this place.*

Our destination, a private club to which June surely belonged, bore her elegant stamp. Even though the rush of this event held a significance not likely to be lost on guests, its execution under her obvious command was flawless.

I stood taking in the ornate room, the servers circulating with champagne flutes and hors d'oeuvres, the big band onstage playing Sinatra, the explosions of flowers at every turn. As I scanned the crowd, the blood in my body rushed to my face.

The men wore a fairly evenhanded mix of tuxedoes and suits like Tim's. But the women—though some wore silk, or sequined, or great, heavy, beaded things—all wore long, formal gowns. Their spectacular jewelry glittered. They were uniformly dazzling.

Only a moment earlier I'd been June Carter in my pink dress. Now I was a woman in an old, cheap sundress. A woman with no sense of occasion, no money. A woman who belonged at a backyard barbeque, but not here.

I stood there, frozen, when suddenly someone seized my shoulders from behind.

I turned. "Glick." We exchanged a quick hug. I introduced him to Tim.

"Crazy, huh?" Glick gestured at the room. "Didn't think *this* would ever happen."

I nodded. Tim smiled politely.

"Actually"—looking at me, Glick took a gulp of champagne—"I thought it would be you. If anyone."

In my peripheral vision, I saw Tim stir.

"But," Glick went on, now in Tim's direction, "his loss, your gain. Right?"

"Glick." My volume startled us all. "Did you bring anybody?"

"I never bring dates to weddings. The girls at these things are nuts." Scanning the place cards arranged on the linen-draped table beside us, he plucked the one with my name on it and inspected it. "You guys are sitting with me." He drained his flute. "We've got a whole Hurley's crowd at our table. Lot of familiar faces. Come on."

Tim and I trailed after him.

When Dutch, his wife, and their entourage entered the ballroom, everyone stood and applauded. I strained to see.

So this is her. She appeared to have issued forth from some formidable bride machine that rendered her both ceramic-fragile and fearsomely beautiful, her cosmetic armor heavy and villainous, her blond hair severely pulled and piled, her small frame wrapped in and trailing yards and yards of ivory silk. When she sat down at the flower-heaped head table, I caught a glimpse of her red-soled stilettos and knew they would have covered my rent.

Out of costume, she was probably actually beautiful. But I couldn't imagine how she looked when she woke up in the morning.

With this lovely apparition floating on his arm, Dutch strode across the room, a monarch crossing a continent. I watched, grappling with this new vision of him.

My Dutch wouldn't have attended such a formal, fussily choreographed event, much less allowed himself to be made the focal point. *Maybe he'll duck out to talk shit and smoke a joint with the waitstaff behind the building—*

No. He obliged the giant spotlight following him, no matter how relentless and searing.

My Dutch didn't perform for anyone, even when called to by etiquette and common decency. *Maybe he'll declare to this entire party that this farce will unfold no further—*

No. In his tuxedo, a large Rolex gleaming on his wrist, a gold band gleaming on his finger, he smiled and smiled for the incessant cameras.

My Dutch did not want to get married or have children. *Maybe I've stumbled into some terrible, prolonged dream—*

No. He stood before them all that day and proclaimed otherwise. We had gathered to raise glasses to this union.

When I tried to integrate my Dutch with the one before me, the reconciliation jumped from my hands, a frantic fish.

"Hey," Tim whispered.

I'd forgotten him. He gestured at my shaking hand, the wine I held sloshing back and forth, threatening to spill. I clicked the glass down on the table.

Before dinner, the maid of honor gave a speech about the bonds of sisterhood. She told the bride she deserved to be treated like a princess, and now she'd found her prince. She dabbed her eyes with a tissue. In his speech, the best man bemoaned how the bride had "picked Dutch off" from their pack. "Never thought I'd see the day, buddy." At his behest, everyone raised glasses for what he called his "fallen brother."

I'd never met this man that I'd heard Dutch talk about, someone he'd known since childhood. I looked around. All the people he'd told me about, the names I'd heard, never connected to faces—they probably filled this room. *Is Jimmy here? Is John?* Surely June would have invited him. Surely this crowd included all of Dutch's hometown friends, all the relatives I had almost met in Memphis. *I've always wanted to meet these people.* Now I never would. I would circulate in the same room as them for one night, a ghost in a crowd.

When I sensed the first dance coming, I sneaked out to smoke by the service entrance. I left again when Dutch and his wife began making their rounds, remembering as I escaped how Fiona and Denny had done the same at their wedding. I didn't possess the grace James had shown that night. Grateful that Glick and the others had absorbed Tim into their group, I took every opportunity to shrink from view or flee.

When I returned to the ballroom after another cigarette, Dutch and his wife were dancing together. For a moment, the crowd around them parted like the sea. For a moment, the only one of the night, he and I made eye contact.

The sudden, full brilliance of day was a shock. Then, just as quickly, I was struck, flying through the dark.

How had I wanted this chance to face him? I stood rooted to the ground, a pale statue in a cheap dress. His wife's hand rested on his bicep as they danced. Seeing the sparkle of the diamond, a giant, ostentatious thing no doubt meant to quiet the skeptics, my thumb found the sapphire on my finger. Now, two women wore his ring.

I spun on my heel and nearly crashed, with the full force of my panic, into someone directly behind me.

"June," I gasped. There she stood, exquisite in strapless royal blue taffeta. "I'm so sorry."

"Don't be." The warmth of her hug surprised me. As we stepped apart, Tim and Glick approached. I introduced them to June, and we stood exchanging pleasantries.

"Great party," Tim enthused.

"I'm so glad you could be here," June demurred. "We have cigar rollers in the lounge if you're interested."

"Let's go!" Glick boomed.

Tim allowed himself to be hauled away, calling over his shoulder to June, "Nice to meet you."

I waited for her to excuse herself. Instead, she stood beside me, surveying Dutch and his wife, the expansive room, full of people.

I felt I should speak. "This really is beautiful."

"Thank you," she said again. "Did you know that the mayor is here?"

"Really?"

"Yes, a number of local politicians, actually. Some big names in the community. Everyone we invited came. I'm so pleased."

Everyone came, everyone who must have scorched her with their murmured judgments during Dutch's trial. I wondered how she felt, looking at them now, assembled to celebrate him.

"I'm sure Dutch told you, they're expecting."

I waited for her to finish her sentence. Then, realizing she had, I stumbled. "Yes. He mentioned it."

"I admit, I was…put off, when I first got the news. I wish they had waited."

I nodded and tried to hide my astonishment at this intimacy.

"But after taking some time to process," she continued, sipping her wine, "I realized this is probably for the best, having a baby first. This way, things are"—she sipped again—"settled."

Oh my God. I sipped my own wine, still nodding in agreement. *June's drunk.*

"He was always so unsettled. He went through so much. I'm sure you know."

I knew. She'd spent all her love, all her resources, all her might, trying to coax the man she loved away from the edge. Then she'd spent her motherhood doing the same. In Dutch, she must have seen a terrifying replica of his father.

I said, "He told me a lot. I hope you don't mind."

"I'm glad he could talk to you like that." She wobbled a little. "And I'll tell you, once life calmed down a bit after his trouble, and he moved away, I was relieved. I felt so guilty about that. But with him two hours away, I got a break from knowing too much and seeing too much. From the constant worry."

There was no doubt that he was, and always had been, absolutely central to her. And now, maybe, he was finally stepping away from the edge.

She gestured at the crowd. "He told me so many times this would never happen. He always told me not to get my hopes up. But I know my son. He just needed time."

We looked at Dutch and his wife on the crowded dance floor, slowing their rotation to smile for a photographer. When I turned my gaze back to June, she looked as if she were releasing a breath she'd been holding for years.

"I thought it might be you," she said, resting her hand on my arm, "but…" She gazed at Dutch, so handsome in his tux, his smile never wavering. "Your Tim seems very nice." She withdrew her hand and motioned toward Dutch's wife. "And she's a good girl. Very grounded. So things have a way of working out."

I scrutinized the front of the voluminous wedding dress, searching for evidence of the life growing there. "Congratulations on the baby," I offered, my voice faint.

"Thank you." June beamed. "I've always wanted a grandchild."

A woman walked up to us, and June introduced me to her

sister Rita, though the sister part was unnecessary. She was practically June's twin, whom I remembered from the family photo Dutch used to keep on his fridge. *Another relative you'll never know.*

June introduced me as an old friend of Dutch's. Maybe she was being pointed, or discreet. Maybe she was simply stating a fact.

Rita shook my hand. "What a sweet little dress."

I gave June a final hug and excused myself. Casting one more look back, I saw June watching Dutch and his wife. I saw guests watching June, standing glittery-eyed at the edge of the dance floor. Some smiled and must have thought they understood: momentous occasion, seeing your child get married. But I saw June's hope, as tremulous and boundless as only a parent's could be, that maybe, maybe, she was witnessing her child's salvation.

12

Presently, we have lunch on a monthly basis, where we talk primarily about family. Drugs and alcohol have no role in this shared time. It is clear to me that now, at forty-four, Dutch is a much different man than he was at twenty-one. Now, his wife, his daughter, and his sobriety are the center of his life.

We didn't meet for lunch. We never met at all. But we were, we agreed, having an affair.

It didn't start that way. I thought he wouldn't contact me again once he got married and the baby arrived. When he did, I felt the same jolt I always had when I looked down at my phone and found him there.

Our reports came in rushes, toppling over and crashing into each other. There remained between us an awe that one's life progressed without the other, a mutual demand for a thorough accounting of the other's time and thoughts and plans, a mutual eagerness to provide it. When these phone calls ended, I lay in bed, unable to sleep, charged by the current of his voice.

Yes, I'm still teaching, I told him when he asked. Still in my apartment, still dating Tim. Still.

"Tim's the guy you told me about before. The one you brought to my wedding."

"That's the one."

"So you've been together, what, two years?"

"About." When he said it, it didn't sound right.

"Must be pretty serious."

"It's not really. But it's going fine." I couldn't recall ever having used the word *fine* to characterize a romantic relationship.

These waters lacked the depth and movement I was used to, but they were calm. I could sometimes, like one morning after

Tim spent the night, even forget the mirror, sitting in front of it but looking out the window instead.

When Tim passed the open bathroom door and saw me there, he paused to watch me. I was perched on the toilet, absently rolling my toothbrush around in my mouth.

I asked through the toothpaste, "Do you need the bathroom?"

"No." He looked sheepish. "Sorry."

He moved as if to leave, then turned back to me. "I like looking at you."

I looked in the mirror at my smeary mouth, my slightly dirty hair, my worn, oversized Fire Department T-shirt.

I looked back at Tim, who said, "You look beautiful."

This is all my fault. I wondered if I was broken.

I told Fiona, "I'm not sure if I just need to know him better, or if I know everything there is to know." I kept searching him for the angles and edges that moved me most. I kept finding only rounded softness.

"You just need to know him better. Lean in," Fiona advised.

Later, as Claire and I sat smoking on my balcony, I asked her, "Does Fiona ever tell you about fights or problems with Denny?"

"Not beyond little day-to-day stuff." She squinted across the street at my neighbor, who was trying to cram more junk into his already bulging garage. "Why?"

"Do you think that's weird?"

"Not really. Not for them. Does she tell you about fights or problems?"

"No. And I think it's weird."

I was being shitty. Claire did not want to be drawn into this conversation. Her look conveyed both. "What should they be fighting about?"

"It's not that." I drew on my cigarette and watched my neighbor. "It's—it's that Fiona never seems to want anything other than exactly what she has."

The want was always with me.

"You guys are just different," Claire said. "With you, it's only love if it hits an artery. With Fiona, it's quieter." She considered. "Calmer."

I blew my smoke out into the treetops. "That doesn't sound like love. That sounds like companionship."

"Well, that's where couples end up. Even if you start out with the intensity, you can't sustain it. No one can."

"Some can. Some do."

Claire arched an eyebrow. "Like who?"

"Johnny Cash and June Carter," I said.

She shook her head. "Name a couple that you know personally."

Me and Dutch. I didn't say it.

"Fiona's wired for quiet," Claire concluded. "And, heads up, I'm pretty sure Tim is too."

Outwardly, Tim and I were a perfectly congruous pair, with our nearly identical backgrounds and overlapping friends and compatible politics and similar taste in books and movies. But our talking had a labored quality that made me long for the click of perfect recognition. *Oh. It's you.*

Dutch seemed relieved that I had so little to report. Hearing myself describe a life that had hardly changed since last we spoke, I felt like a failure.

Fiona and Denny, like all my friends who now had kids, jogged at a steady clip between the obligations of work and family life. James, our perpetual Peter Pan, had announced that he would be the new co-owner of Ginty's.

"I've been saving for this and working on my uncle for a long time to bring me on," he told us. "Time for a paycheck with a comma in it."

Even Claire, who for years had focused on her career, told me out of the blue, "I'm seeing someone."

"Since when?"

Since the last month, she said. When I pressed her for details, she offered only a few. His name was Julian. They worked together. He was also in management, and a little older.

I waited for her sarcasm. I waited for a dry prediction of the relationship's demise or a dismissive comment about a fling. Instead, she let slip a small, private smile.

Oh my god. I smiled back and stopped pressing. I couldn't remember seeing Claire so taken.

I'd seemingly stood still while the lives of everyone around me had changed. And Dutch's most of all. I could hardly process the things he told me. "I still can't believe you're married."

In my parents' yard, two trees stood side by side. Over time they bent more and more toward each other, and I sometimes found my parents standing before the trees, studying them.

"I don't want to cut down either one," my mom said.

My dad stroked his face, mulling. "Maybe we could move one."

"No." She shook her head. "I'm afraid it would die."

Eventually, they gave up the idea of intervention, and the branches became so entangled and entwined that the trees fused, indistinguishable from each other, impossible to separate without doing harm. The trees reminded me of my parents.

"Old school" was how I'd always described their marriage to Claire and Fiona. "It's generational." People our age might have chafed under such interdependence and longed for more autonomy. But as the years ticked by and some of my parents' friends divorced, mine continued to stretch and bend toward each other.

All year they looked forward to their annual winter trip to Florida with lifelong friends. When they returned, I tried to be patient while they showed me endless stacks of printed pictures that they then placed in albums: their group clustered together on a golf course, on a beach, in front of some restaurant, on a deck with glasses raised, the ocean sparkling behind them. In every picture, they were beaming.

Then last winter, my mom slipped on some ice. She broke her ankle. As the three of us sat at the kitchen table, she announced that for the first time in the history of their Florida tradition, she would skip the trip. "It would be too much. And I would just slow everyone down."

"I'll stay here with Mom while you're gone," I said to my dad.

He shook his head. "I'm not going either."

"You should go, Dave," my mom said.

"You should go, Dad," I echoed. "I promise I'll take good care of her."

After a week of arguing about it, I gave up. For my dad, taking the trip without my mom was unthinkable.

I couldn't imagine Dutch doing that. But what he described to me—the TV shows his wife had gotten him to watch, the couch they picked out together, the time they spent with "their" friends, who used to be her friends—suggested that he was doing exactly that. I listened, incredulous.

"And you're a dad now," I said to him again and again. When I tried to bend my mind around it, it always circled back to Fiona and Denny.

I thought of how, when Fiona got pregnant the first time, she and Denny rearranged all their priorities. How they vanished from the bar. How with Liam's birth, and again with Maggie's, their surrender to sleep deprivation was immediate, a matter of fact. How they wrapped themselves around their kids like vines.

Every St. Patrick's Day, James invited all of our friends to Ginty's. The coveted pocket of space he saved for us served as our home base, which we safeguarded and returned to throughout the day to warm up, drink more beer, eat, and listen to the bands. Fiona and Denny skipped the festivities when their kids were really little, but this year, they showed up with Liam and Maggie in tow.

"You brought the kids." James couldn't hide his dismay.

Denny smiled and shrugged. Fiona said cheerfully, "Yep. We have kids."

Throughout the day, I watched my friends chase after them, herd them to and from the bathroom, entertain them, wipe their perpetually sticky faces and fingers, add and subtract their coats, snow pants, mittens, hats. At night, the kids climbed onto their parents' laps.

I watched as Liam and Maggie, who had not stopped moving all day, stilled. Their eyes became hooded. In the middle of a boisterous crowd, they both fell asleep, Liam draped across his mom, Maggie wilted against her dad's shoulder. As they fastened their arms around their kids like seatbelts, Fiona and Denny shared a look of total contentment.

I couldn't imagine Dutch doing that. But as he described wrestling his daughter into tiny dresses and tights, stripping her and starting over when she vomited down the front of herself, taking her on long, meandering drives to lull her to sleep, it sounded like he was doing exactly that.

I asked him, "Can I see a picture?"

"Yeah. But"—he hesitated—"she's in all of them." She was his wife. "You sure?"

I figured that if I could take a punch, I could take a bullet. "Yeah. Send them."

"Hang on." Two minutes later, my phone chimed. I stared at the pictures of his wife, smiling and clutching his child.

Stripped of her frightening bridal adornments, she was no longer the nearly mythical creature from the reception, but pleasantly, unremarkably pretty. Nothing about her suggested the supernatural.

I leaned in for a closer look. *She must like pink.* She was wearing it in almost every picture.

The baby looked just like him. "The spit of him," my parents would have said. Dutch explained that because his wife was over forty when she got pregnant, and because both the pregnancy and delivery were harrowing, her parents, who had long given up hope of a grandchild, referred to the little girl as "the miracle baby."

I thought again of my parents. *We can't wait for your wains.* They had said it my whole adult life, and at forty-three, I tried to remember the last time they had said it, and couldn't.

I'm never having kids. Dutch had said it so many times throughout our relationship. And when he leaned toward me, leaned toward me so much so that I thought he might alter his course for me, and might want to, he had always said it again.

Looking at the little girl in the pictures, I couldn't help a small, bitter smile. Miracle baby, indeed.

Years ago, when Dutch and I were together, I'd said to Claire, "No one can look at someone else's relationship and fully see it." But I had believed for years, based on a handful of stories and a movie, that I understood Johnny Cash and June Carter's relationship.

What could I have possibly understood about the real people, beyond two actors' depictions of them onscreen? It was their performance I loved, beautifully edited and polished and closed on such a satisfying note that I forgave any liberties taken with the truth.

So it was entirely possible, I reasoned, returning to the pictures Dutch sent, that the images and anecdotes he shared illuminated nothing. Maybe, as he always said, he truly was incapable of being a family man, beyond the title and technicality and presentation of such. Maybe his wife experienced the same detachment I had, all those years ago, and felt at times like a widow. Maybe his daughter would grow up feeling fatherless, as Dutch himself had.

Or maybe—my mind flipped like a coin—maybe he had been perfectly capable all along. Just not with me.

Then one night, as I lay in bed, thinking of him, he texted me. *Do you ever wear your ring?* I almost laughed out loud. *Ever.* I turned and twisted the ever-present sapphire on my finger, my pulse quickening, his step toward me unmistakable.

Yes.

I wavered, thinking. Then I tapped out another message.

Did you keep my letters?

I watched the ellipses dance on the screen of my phone, and then vanish. My phone chimed.

Yes.

The next night, after another lengthy conversation, my phone chimed. *Do you remember the cottage?* Another step. I stared at his text, deliberating. And in a surge of abandon, the necessary kind that made lengthy, yearning silences bearable, I took not a step but a leap. *We woke up in the sand, covered in ladybugs... you said they were good luck... I took you in my mouth... we closed our eyes and listened to the surf.*

And we were bounding toward each other all over again.

The fevered momentum of our conversations would culminate in a face-to-face meeting, I thought, imagining it in a dark, elegant hotel bar. To any onlooker, our electrified exchange would be indistinguishable from the soft chorus of murmurs and clinking wine glasses and tinkling piano. Then, the elevator, Dutch lifting me against its walls, frantic tongues and hands. Finally, a spare but beautiful hotel room, overlooking the night-lit city and neon-painted river below us as we panted and locked together, the full expression of years of want.

We didn't meet. We talked incessantly for a year, at night, when his wife had gone to bed and Tim had left town for work. The ease of our treachery surprised us.

Playgroups, lunch dates, dinner parties, vacations: he said these pastimes occupied his wife and that infidelity would never even occur to her.

"Are you sure? You make her sound like an imbecile."

"It's not that. It's more like, as long as everything looks the way she wants it to, she's happy."

"Sounds like Tim. They'd probably be really compatible." Then I asked, "Does she know about you?" I wondered if he understood my question.

"She knows some things." He understood me. "But she doesn't want to know more than absolutely necessary." He paused. "I've tried at different points to tell her things. But when I do, she shakes her head and says, 'No, no, no' and covers her ears."

I pictured Dutch's wife doing this, like a child.

In some conversations, he was still the person I'd always known, making me laugh, throwing grenades, asking which movies I was watching so he could watch them too. But the conversations could turn so fast.

My Dutch had loved watching ballgames from the nose-bleed seats, drinking cheap beer in the sun. "This is just hair and teeth," he'd once said between bites of a stadium hot dog. "I think that makes it vegetarian."

When we were first dating, I had mentioned one night that wine sounded good. He dashed out to get it for me. When he returned from the store and poured some, I smiled and thanked him, though the liquid in my glass came from a cardboard box and looked like Kool Aid. Now he told me about standing in the cellar of the home that he and his wife paid other people to clean, deliberating over which bottles to pair with dinner.

My Dutch had cycled through a fixed rotation of fraying T-shirts, jeans, and ball caps, insisting that only years of wear broke them in properly. Now he told me that he and his wife each had a closet the size of a bedroom. She had filled his with clothes she selected, every piece emblazoned with the designer names she loved most.

My Dutch had wanted and welcomed my warm imprint on his house. He bought the candles and feathery mounds of bedding that I liked. He turned off ESPN and turned on music I chose. We painted his living room together. Now he listed the things in his house that he was not allowed to touch and the furniture on which he was not allowed to sit.

"Who *are* you?" I asked him, and he laughed off my question. His reports sounded like dispatches from a country neither of us would have ever visited. Now, he lived there.

His desire to tell me about their house bewildered me at first. He brought it up in several times, always with the preface, "You know Forest Hills, right?"

Along with everyone else in town, I was familiar. Though the neighborhood was gated, Forest Hills was neither wooded nor hilly and therefore visible from the main roads that enclosed it. Its inhabitants loved to drop this brand name, their small smiles and lowered gazes feigning modesty and mild embarrassment. Then they waited for the usual breathy reverence and prickling envy. Picturing Dutch living there with his wife and child, I wanted to smash glass.

The square footage and prices of the houses rivaled each other in monstrosity, but they were uniformly beige and dull, hardly distinguishable from one another. Though pools and tennis courts abounded, I had never once, driving past, observed any of them in use.

I faced no danger of having to decide what to do with an exorbitant amount of money. But if I had, I couldn't imagine choosing to spend it on a hulking, soulless beige box.

"Tell me more, Dutch." I didn't even try to force the frost from my voice. "Tell me all about the house you and your wife share. Describe for me in detail your bedroom and the wedding portrait over the mantel."

"There's no wedding portrait over the mantel."

I could hardly stand the thought of him married to someone else. Listening to him describe their home, I wondered if he wanted to rub my face in shit.

Then one night, he told me about a new pool table he had ordered. "You would love it. Remember how we used to play all the time?"

All at once, the anger drained from me. He had sought my approval when we were dating. And this whole business of talking about his house, though almost laughably obtuse, suddenly seemed like that need showing itself again.

I trolled Forest Hills real estate online. The pictures suggested that after the initial satisfaction of their purchase, owners panicked at the realization that they must actually fill all that empty space. Then they made a series of identical decisions: hanging massive, ornately framed paintings, not for the art itself but to occupy all those vast stretches of blank wall; installing plush home theatres and state-of-the-art gyms that no one would visit; devoting an entire room to the display of a single object, like a baby grand piano no one knew how to play. Or a pool table.

"What do you think of Forest Hills?" pressed Dutch, his vulnerability almost naked.

What did it matter? None of it was mine. None of it was ours.

I didn't want to hurt him. I didn't want to lie. "I think you really like it, and I think that's great."

Sometimes, I heard the lethargy of his wealth. He said he was thinking about putting in a pool. He said he might buy a boat. When I suggested, "You could get a boat and drive it around your pool," he didn't laugh.

Sometimes his tone deafness stunned me, and my flare of anger surprised us both. When he told me the college-sized price tag on the preschool his daughter would be attending, he was as nonchalant as if telling me what he ate for dinner. When he told me his wife had just picked up her new BMW, I asked, "What happened to the old one?"

"Nothing. She just got tired of it."

During this conversation I was seated at my kitchen table. On it, face down, I had placed a mechanic's estimate for new brakes. I couldn't look at it until I knew how I would pay for it.

I said to Dutch, "This is why rich people can only be friends with other rich people. They can't relate to anyone else."

A brief silence followed. He sounded injured. "I'm talking to you about my life. That's what we do."

Where are you, Dutch? There, opening between us, the canyon I'd feared ever since the money came.

"I have to go," I said, and hung up before he could respond.

13

The particulars of Dutch's marriage littered our conversations. I couldn't escape them.

He told me about their recent stay at June's house, the crisis of discovering they had left all their daughter's pacifiers behind, the hunt for a twenty-four-hour store that sold them as the baby wailed in the back seat, his wife's argument with her mother. The names of in-laws sounded as easy and comfortable in his mouth as those of his own family.

He spent a Saturday trailing after a professional photographer, hired by his wife to take family portraits. For hours he tried to smile through the suffocation of his too-tight dress-shirt collar as the photographer arranged and endlessly rearranged them together in her studio, in front of a fountain in a park, in their own lush backyard.

"It was exhausting. This marriage is exhausting," he concluded. "I made such a mistake."

"Yes," I said. "You did." I refused to console him for marrying the wrong person. Only after our call ended did I realize that the "mistake" could have meant either the photo shoot or marriage in general.

Sometimes, when I couldn't tolerate these snapshots of mundane, entwined married life anymore, I changed the subject. But sometimes I pressed him for more details. I couldn't help myself. I had to know.

"You did what you said you would never do," I said one night. "You tied your life to hers. She must have been something to you that no one else was."

"She was. Pregnant. And you have to remember, we'd only been together a few months at that point. We barely knew each other."

"You didn't have to get married just because of a pregnancy."

"You know how conservative my family is. Hers is too. I think we both felt like we had to."

I remained quiet.

"What?" he prodded.

"Getting married just because someone's pregnant—teenagers in the fifties did that. But forty-year-olds with plenty of resources don't. Not now. Not unless they want to." I took a slow lap around my living room. "You must have really loved her. You 'loved her deeply.' That's what you said." I never forgot those words.

"I loved you. I still do."

I let this declaration cascade over me. My next question clanged with futility. "What do you think would've happened if she'd never gotten pregnant?"

"I know exactly what would've happened. We would've run our course and moved on."

I fidgeted. "But you said when you told me she was pregnant that you would've gotten married anyway. That you had already talked about marriage."

"What? No," he scoffed. "I never would have said that." He reconsidered. "Or if I did, I was drunk. Or it just seemed like the right thing to say at the time, since it was a shotgun wedding. But I don't think I said that."

Whether he had truly loved his wife in the beginning or felt himself tethered to her, I couldn't know. But I came to realize at least one reason his marriage held value.

The answer was not in the pictures he sent, though I expected to find it there and obsessed over his wife's image. It could be found in our almost nightly conversations. His wife had something to offer that I never had.

Before her, Dutch's social circle had consisted mostly of guys like him, fixtures at dive bars who watched baseball and played Keno. Even after the money came, that humble sphere remained his comfort zone and refuge, where his wife's friends, wealthy without exception, wouldn't deign to enter.

According to Dutch, they were seasoned entrepreneurs,

successful business owners, Ivy Leaguers, trust-fund kids. They vacationed together in Europe and the Caribbean and were charmed to learn, before their first group trip, that Dutch had applied for his first passport.

Their dinner parties became competitions to determine who among them served or brought the best scotches and wines, the hardest to find and the most coveted. Their nights out included the best restaurants, where they knew the owners, who ushered them into private rooms and fawned over them like royalty.

I imagined Dutch seated at these tables. Anyone trying to lord their wealth over him, he would simply out-buy, relishing the challenge. But among people so invested in outdoing and impressing one another, the ones with gilded degrees surely brandished them. They surely asked him about his own education and found his answer amusing. *What does he do then?*

Picturing it, part of me wanted to rush the imaginary room and save him from it. Part of me wanted to save his wife from what he surely took out on her afterward.

I asked him, "What do you all talk about?"

Over extravagant meals, they gossiped and discussed their investments. They planned their next trip. They crowed over the procurement of some new, elusive, spectacularly expensive item, a particular watch or handbag or car, often bypassing long wait lists in the process. No door was closed to them.

These descriptions agitated and depressed me. "So no one has kids." I swallowed. "Except you."

"Everyone has kids."

They never cropped up in his stories. "Where are all the kids?"

He said, as if saying the sky was up, "Everyone has a nanny."

He had already been rich when he met his wife. She taught him how to be rich.

Disquiet trailed behind me, tripping me. I couldn't pinpoint the source. Dutch told me that in addition to traveling with this circle, he and his wife also saw them two or three times a week.

I said, "Most of my friends are too busy with their careers and families to get out much, maybe once or twice a month." In my twenties, my friends and I were inseparable. This dynamic among people in their forties struck me as odd.

"I know, but with these people," he explained, "there's always a trip or a party or an event. Everyone goes. You have to."

I twisted my ring. "You *have* to?"

"I do. It's expected."

But Dutch had never done what others expected of him if he didn't want to. In our four years as a couple, he had interacted with my friends and family only a handful of times. Remembering this rejection of my friends, the kind who dug through snow with their bare hands to look for a lost ring, the sting felt fresh.

Is that it? Maybe this nagging nuisance was plain jealousy that he gave his wife what he never wanted to give me. Maybe he had learned to set his own wants aside to prioritize someone else's. Maybe her friends so dazzled him that he invited and welcomed their steady presence.

We talked the night before one of his trips to Mexico. Knowing I wouldn't hear his voice again for ten days, I masked my bleakness with a joke. "Maybe when you're all parasailing, your wife will take a little spill and get eaten by a shark."

"No chance of that. All we do on these trips is drink."

The knot of unrest came undone and stretched before me, a simple rope.

I couldn't believe I hadn't untied it sooner. Alcohol was the centerpiece of their time together, of these relationships. It surged through their endless gatherings, even their children's lavish birthday parties. *There's always a trip, a party, an event. Everyone goes. You have to.* Nothing better suited an addict than the constant company of other addicts, who normalized and sanctioned the excesses.

When he had first described his new life to me, it sounded so different from his former life with the Keno crowd. Now I realized that only the scenery had changed, elegantly reframed, dive bars replaced with opulent homes and restaurants, Jim Beam and Budweiser with aged single malt and vintage Opus One.

When he was somewhat drunk, Dutch talked about our future in conditional hypotheticals: what we would relearn about each other, where we would travel together, where we would live. But one night, he asked me, "Where will we live?" *Will*, not *would*. He was very drunk.

I said, "We could probably squeeze your pool table into my apartment."

"Stop. I'm serious." On the other end, I heard the *thup* of a popped cork. "Where do you want to live?"

What did it matter? I knew, once Dutch ended the call and crawled into bed next to his wife, that I would pay for indulging this dreamy speculation.

But as he prodded me, I thought of Johnny Cash and June Carter's home in Tennessee. The rambling Hendersonville house overlooking a wooded lake, initially his alone, the place where she lifted him out of the muddy water and into involuntary detox, became the beloved backdrop of their marriage.

"You know, I read a lot on my balcony," I hedged. "And when I look out, I see my shirtless eighty-year-old neighbor and his hoarded garage."

Dutch laughed, as I'd wanted him to. "And so?"

"So it would be nice to look out and see something else." My sincerity was creeping in. "Like water."

"And?"

"And…hills. Woods."

"What else?" His voice, I thought right then, would be the end of me.

"Or…" I balked, then gave myself over to the fantasy and accepted the price. "A house with some history, some personality." Not Forest Hills, not some nouveau-riche new build. A stately old house, vines climbing the red brick. The sparkle and warm glow of colored leaded glass and crystals dripping from bronze light fixtures. The intricacies of hundred-year-old woodwork. A staircase that curved like a dancer's arm. Sunlight streaming in through an abundance of tall, arched windows.

The first time Dutch took me to the cottage, I felt that a person like me had no business in a place that beautiful, unless perhaps to clean it. Now I tried to imagine sharing a place like that with him, a place we would learn to refer to as "ours," a place where I actually belonged.

"What else?" he asked.

"Or, something simple." A memory came to me. "Like that Cape Cod around the block from my old place, the one with the pink garden. It went up for sale when we were first dating."

"It was pretty small. We could do better." Conditional.

"It was small." Some houses were designed so that their occupants never had to encounter one another. But that house would fill with the smell of my dark coffee brewing, his body-wash after a shower, fresh basil for pesto. It would fill with music we picked out together, a steady soundtrack to our clattering and rustles.

Dutch said, "I could give you any of this, or all of it." Conditional. "I'll give you whatever you want." Future.

"That's all just geography, though. It doesn't matter." I was already on my knees; I thought I might as well lie down. "All I ever really wanted was you."

We had stumbled past the house with the pink garden so many years ago. Afterward he hadn't remembered saying to me, "We could live here together. If you'll have me." And that night, climbing into bed alone, I knew he wouldn't remember that conversation either.

He would not see me. I searched my reflection for the reason, searched the pictures we'd shared. When he asked, I sent only one, agonizing over its selection.

Tim had taken the picture at a recent party. I was standing a few feet away from him with friends. My distance from the camera softened and forgave the small lines on my face, lines that Dutch's wife and her friends would pay doctors to smooth away with injections. I was wearing heels and makeup and looked lean. I was laughing at something someone had said. When Tim sent it to me, a one-word text message accompanied it. *Beautiful.*

I held my breath as I sent it to Dutch, then exhaled when he responded. "You look the same."

So did he. Like mine, his eyes showed slight weathering. Like mine, the faint crease on his forehead would deepen with time. Years of drawing on cigarettes had formed the beginnings of parentheses at the sides of his mouth. But time had not thickened him, diminished his shoulders, or chased away his hairline. In these pictures, I detected no noteworthy physical decline in either of us that might create reservations about meeting.

Maybe, then, he preferred me as an idea. Maybe he kept it all separate and manageable by maintaining one uncrossed line. We remained, to each other, disembodied voices.

"Remember that letter you wrote me," he asked one night, "that described driving around with your friend in high school?"

I remembered.

"Let's do that. Let's get a 'vette and go, you and me. Let's just drive."

I said, "Let's go."

"I'll be right over."

If he got in his car, right then, and came to me, I thought, he would have actually been right over. He lived only a few minutes away.

But we might as well have lived on different continents. We shared a silence.

I asked, no longer in reference to a fantastical escape in a sports car, "Are you coming?" He understood me. I could tell by his rustling. I tried again. My voice changed. "Are you coming?"

"I want to."

The anguish leapt out before I could stop it. "I've been waiting for you for eleven years."

He was always there and never there. I couldn't have him or mourn him. And so I was not well or sick, but held by a persistent, dull aching, the kind a person became accustomed to, the kind a person learned to tolerate.

Sometimes he said with great urgency that he must see me. We planned a day, time, and place. Anticipation coursed through me, making eating and sleeping impossible. And each time he canceled, citing some unforeseeable last-minute crisis. The disappointment so crushed me, the adrenaline draining from me in such a flood, that I wilted.

I pored over pictures of Dutch's wife. She had Dutch. She shared his name, his child, his life. *Does she feel lucky?*

Maybe. But maybe ceaseless attempts to reach the sandbars exhausted her. Maybe she had to learn and relearn the terrible deception in their distance. Maybe, every time she looked in the mirror, failure looked back at her.

The smallest whisper stirred beneath my mountainous longing to see Dutch. *This is her problem now.*

Each year at the end of October, my town held a fair, a final gasp in the sun. Knowing it was about to retreat behind the cast-iron clouds of advancing winter, everyone came, cramming the fair's six blocks through the weekend. I joined Fiona and her kids there on a Saturday, to wait in lines for tickets, carnival rides, games, face painting, paper baskets of greasy fried food, cups of hot chocolate and apple cider.

The line for the twirling teacup ride snaked around the corner. Maggie practically vibrated with anticipation, and our little group shuffled forward, leaves crunching underfoot and skittering around us. When at last we neared the front of the line, Liam announced, "I have to go to the bathroom."

"Liam." Fiona was exasperated. "I just took you."

"I know, but I have to go again." He hopped from foot to foot.

I stayed in line with Maggie as the crowd swallowed Fiona and Liam. Maggie wanted to sit in the flowered purple teacup. So did another little girl. They faced each other, eyes narrowed.

"You can share it," I said, herding the girls into the teacup together. Then I joined the other adults crowding the gated perimeter.

As I idled there, smiling and waving each time Maggie twirled past, I sipped my cider and looked around. Some people rolled strollers back and forth in place, trying to soothe the occupants. Some tried to prevent their restless dogs from entangling themselves in their leashes. Some did both. The parents of these kids, they all smiled and waved. They all furiously snapped pictures.

Suddenly I heard an unmistakably clear voice. *You're never going to have this.*

I didn't know where the voice had come from. The force of it blindsided me.

Where did the possibility go? Maggie twirled by in her teacup. Maybe time took it. Maybe Dutch took it. Maybe I gave it away.

Standing there in a little patch of cheerful afternoon sunshine, the air around me soared with singsong carnival music, the whir of carnival rides, the delighted shrieks of children. Maggie's face blurred before me.

14

Winter came early, its sudden ferocity a jolt. The trees had not shed their leaves before ice encased them and snow weighted them. Then one morning after another early, heavy snowfall, as I looked out my window, drinking coffee and debating how much extra time to allow for my commute, my mom called.

So my caller ID said, but the voice on the other end was so small and strange and far away. "Can you meet me at St. Raphael?"

I couldn't breathe. "What happened?"

"Dad died."

Dad died. The words played on a loop as I drove to the hospital, stupefied. *Dad died.* The words bounced and jangled, an incomprehensible foreign language.

He'd had a heart attack while shoveling, said my mom. A nurse steered me to her in a tiny, windowless room and hurried out. We clutched each other in shared disbelief. Wasn't that just like my dad to be out there charging at the snow before anyone else, the unrelenting scrape of the shovel against concrete probably waking the whole street?

"Dad, why don't you wait a little while?" I used to ask him when he began some noisy outdoor task before eight a.m. This longstanding habit made me laugh through my hands. "The poor neighbors."

That was his way. He was so industrious. And now he was gone.

"Who knows?" I asked my mom.

"Just you."

We pulled out our phones and started making dazed calls. I made one to Tim, who was out of town but told me he would find the next flight home.

Back at the house, here came the relatives and Fiona and Claire. Here came the parish priest and my parents' neighbors. Here came their friends from the League and their bowling team and church. The stream was continuous.

Some came to sit, offering quiet proximity. Some came armed with brown paper bags that shifted and clinked with bottles of liquor and beer. Some came determined to complete some chore. They bustled about cooking food no one wanted, generating dishes that needed washing, making tea.

When my dad's brothers headed outside to finish the job he'd started, I followed them. The previous night's storm had dropped several inches of snow, dazzling then, almost blinding. The sky was technicolor blue. The sun, hardly more than a watermark the past few days, was suddenly an almost comical banana yellow, shining down on the precise location of my dad's death, marked in three places.

One was where he had dropped the shovel, and where it remained. Another, an abrupt line dividing the cleared from the buried sidewalk. The last, the imprint of his body in the snow, an adult-sized snow angel.

Who—I almost laughed at the petty thought—who would shovel the snow now? Who would cut the grass and hang the Christmas lights? Who would do the innumerable household repairs and tasks my mom and I never thought about? Surely, he would be back anytime. Surely it was all some dreadful mistake.

I wanted to stand on the site and gaze at it. I wanted to lie down in his indentation and try to feel him there, discover how quickly the cold of the snow enveloped me. Did it happen fast? Did he call out? I couldn't bear the thought of him lying there, for even a second, cold.

My uncles hurried to work, obliterating the site.

That night, Claire and Fiona collected a duffel bag of essentials from my apartment and brought it to me. Then, because my mom wouldn't, I shooed everyone out. The two of us huddled together in the dim living room, lit only by a small lamp on a side table. Next to it sat his empty recliner.

Because my dad would have, after dinner, I clicked on the TV. The volume and auctioneer-style car dealership commercial made me jump, and I clicked it off. The silence engulfed us.

Where is Dad? I realized I was waiting for him. *Where could he possibly be, at night, without Mom?*

Every week before she shopped for groceries, he told her not to buy ice cream. She rolled her eyes as she left. Then that night or the next, he inevitably sprang from his recliner, left the house, and returned a few minutes later with ice cream.

"Dave." This always exasperated my mom. "I'll just get it when I buy groceries."

"No." He was adamant. "I don't want it in the house." As he settled into his recliner with his spoon and pint of mint chocolate chip, he looked so blissful that I could imagine him as a little boy. *Maybe Dad has run up to the store—*

No.

He was always helping the neighbors. We'd hear a light, apologetic knock at the door, which he opened, then an explanation of the situation. This one needed to borrow jumper cables, that one couldn't get his snow blower started. *Maybe some knock came, and Dad went down the street to—*

No.

His outdoor projects never ended, even in the winter. We watched him out there in the cold and tried to coax him in, but he wouldn't come till he was finished. *Maybe I'll hear the garage door close, and there he'll be in the kitchen, stomping and brushing snow from his Arctic layers—*

No.

My mom broke the silence. Like on the phone that morning—*Was it only this morning? Is that right?*—her voice sounded like a stranger's. "I feel like he's going to walk in any minute."

For four nights I moved back into my childhood bedroom. On the first, I heard my phone ring around eleven and realized I hadn't seen or thought of it in hours. When I found it on the old oak desk in the den, it was Dutch calling. For the first time in fifteen years, for one day, I had forgotten him.

He asked if I'd heard of some documentary he'd just finished watching. I responded, "My dad died." Although I had said the words many times that day, they remained nonsensical and gluey in my mouth.

Like everyone I called that morning, Dutch followed his brief, astounded silence with a series of sputtering questions and condolences. Then he said, "I'll come to the funeral. I want to come. Do you want me to come?"

Yes, I said, I wanted him to come. "Please come." He said that he would, that he'd sit in the back and slip out at the end, but that I would look out and find him there, for me.

So he would, I noted in my submerged, stunned way, make some exceptions after all. We would meet after all. But rather than any of the hundreds of clandestine scenarios I had imagined, we would meet in a crowd, gathered by death.

During the day the house bulged, and I wished everyone would leave. At night a thick, unnerving silence settled over it, and I wished they would all come back. After my mom and I said goodnight, we always found each other again.

When I padded down the hall and found her in her bedroom, sitting on the edge of the bed, I slipped in and sat down beside her. When I wandered into the living room and turned on the TV, she appeared on the couch beside me. When we both found ourselves in the kitchen for no reason, we made tea. Sleep was an impossibility.

In the morning, people reappeared, breaking the spell, filling the house with noise and activity. I watched Aunt Maeve, sitting beside my mom in the den, help her make arrangements with the funeral home and the church. I watched Aunt Peggy, impressively brisk and efficient, dust and scrub bathrooms and gather up laundry. I heard my mom say to someone on the phone, "One second, please." Then she called out, "Peg?"

My aunt paused in the den doorway, and I heard my mom again, her voice faint. "Not our sheets. Please."

She didn't want the smell of him washed away.

At night, I passed through the still house without aim, pausing to examine things: a framed photo of me with a hideous perm and my parents at my high school graduation, the mail, shoved into the slot and forgotten, my dad's ancient, chocolate-colored leather wallet on the kitchen counter, the doorframe where he had recorded my height throughout the years with a series of pencil marks and dates.

I moved to the living room and climbed into his recliner, momentarily comforted by its familiar squeak and worn armrests. This was as close as I could get to my dad now, I thought, as close as I'd ever get again. But a fear came, that my imprint and smell would displace his, and I sprang to my feet.

I wandered into the dark kitchen, opened the refrigerator, and stood in its ghostly light, contemplating the bulging abundance of its contents and the determination of whoever had packed it. I wandered into the bathroom and picked up my dad's razor and toothbrush. I noted the new bar of Zest soap in the soap dish and its twin in the shower.

For my whole life and most of his, my dad had worn the same tidy crew cut and washed his hair with a bar of Zest. My mom and I had teased him endlessly about this, but he saw no need for frivolous extras like shampoo. "The Zest takes care of everything," he said. He prided himself on his utilitarian, five-minute showers.

Then one Christmas, when the whole family had crammed into our living room to distribute and tear into presents, my cousin Katie presented my dad with a small pink gift bag. It bore the name, in scrolling gold script, of the salon where she worked.

He removed the jaunty flourish of polka-dotted tissue paper, peered into the bag, and drew from it a plastic tube. "What is it?"

"It's product," Katie explained. "It'll give your hair a more textured look."

Picturing the bewilderment on his face then, looking at the bar of Zest, I laughed out loud. It bounced against the tiles.

On my way out of the bathroom, I paused at the medicine cabinet and opened it. On a glass shelf sat an orange plastic bottle of oxycodone. Though the label had faded, my mom's name was still legible.

The crowded house allowed me to observe my mom from an inconspicuous distance. Everyone was watching her, and I wondered if the sight of her, suddenly without my dad and suddenly frail, jarred them too.

People noticed when spouses in their company fatigued and aggravated each other. They also noticed when spouses like my parents, despite their almost sitcomish bickering, felt truly at ease only when together. People scarcely saw or thought of my parents separately, and evidence of this surrounded me in snatches of overheard conversations. "DaveandMaura. DaveandMaura." I was shocked at how my mom moved around the house, talking and breathing, suddenly missing half of herself.

When people approached to hug me, check on me, or stand with me, pensive, most of their stories referred to one entity. "Yourmomanddad. Yourmomanddad." Those who spoke of him as an individual said, again and again, "He was one of my best friends."

What a remarkable thing. All of them claimed this closeness. All of them were right.

Late at night, at the kitchen table with my mom, I remembered the plastic bottle. "Why do you have oxycodone, Mom?"

A crease formed between her eyebrows. "What is that?"

I retrieved the bottle from the bathroom and handed it to her. She looked it over, unsure. Then, "I know. I got those after I broke my ankle."

"But you never took them." The bottle was full.

"Just for the first day. I didn't like how they made me feel."

"How did they make you feel?"

"Oh—" She waved at the air. "Like a cow in a field, staring off into space."

"Mom." I headed to bed, chuckling. As soon as my head hit the pillow, the lightness transformed into a heavy, monstrous aching. What would she have given then to feel nothing?

What had Dutch said once about pills? I stared up at the ceiling. He took them because he didn't want to feel anything at all. That was the point.

The ceiling still bore the speckled, sticky stars I had applied as a kid. Staring up at this constellation, I replayed the night Dutch had filled his house with strangers. I remembered how the seemingly sudden presence of pills had disoriented me, how he threw me out when I pushed him about it, how grateful I was when the fight ended. I had never pushed again.

I replayed the times Dutch had dropped me, his total detachment. The last time, his vacant gaze hardly flickered away from the TV as I moved weeping toward the door. I had described it to Fiona then as his ability to flip some internal switch. Another apt description, I realized that night, was my mom's. Like a cow in a field, staring off into space.

He told me in the very beginning that pills turned off feeling. What had he said? I tossed in the twin bed. *There's nothing better.*

I had always thought alcohol made us a trio. I tossed and turned. Maybe we had been a foursome all along.

The day before the funeral, people stood and sat where they could in small knots around the house, drinking and talking, and the mood—I looked around, startled—felt almost festive. The scene felt like one of the many parties my parents had hosted over the years, as if my dad had run out for more ice, as if everything was fine. Someone somewhere laughed. I stood in a circle with Tim and my friends as James told us about a recent date.

"She was *so* hot. But we were talking, you know, and I don't remember how this even came up, but"—he hesitated a little—"she didn't know what 9/11 was."

"Wait." Claire made the time-out signal. "What?"

"I mean she just didn't know. I brought it up for some reason, I can't remember why, and she didn't know what I was talking about."

We stared at him.

He continued, "I get it, though. I mean, she was only a little kid when it happened."

We stood there doing the mental math. Claire looked so incredulous, and James so sheepish, that I erupted in laughter. Everyone did. And everything *was* fine, and we were at a party. And then my parents' landline rang, and I watched my mom cross the kitchen to answer it, inadvertently hitting the speaker-phone button in the process. Dorothy from Joe's Shoe Repair was calling about the boots.

Over the course of many years, my dad had worn his work boots down to tatters. The laces disintegrated. The leather tore. The soles peeled away. Each time it seemed he would finally pronounce them unsalvageable, he took them to Joe's and waited for their return, prompting my mom to say, "You should throw those out."

"Maura, you don't throw something away just because of a little wear and tear." He waved the repaired boots at her. "Good as new."

"They're disgusting. You could have bought twenty new pairs of boots with all the money you've spent at Joe's."

Then he gave the speech. "Maura. These are my *work* boots. I *love* these boots. One day, I want to be buried in these boots."

Dorothy chirped that the boots were ready to be picked up, adding, "Hi to Dave."

My mom hung up and started to cry, only it didn't sound like crying but like an animal being strangled. And the reason for our assembly rushed back to me, and it was not a party. *Dad died.*

My aunts rushed to her, patting her and entreating her to rest and eat and "take a break." How could she take a break from the amputation of half of herself? They were so well-meaning and helpless.

I went with my mom to Joe's. We picked up the boots and took them to the funeral home. And the next morning when we stood together in the church vestibule, looking at him one last time before the coffin was closed, he was wearing the suit my mom had selected and his work boots.

His wedding ring, a plain gold band, swayed on a delicate chain around my mom's neck. It was much too big for her finger. Now, we both wore rings of the missing.

The pallbearers carried the coffin down the center aisle. Throughout the Mass, my gaze returned to it. I couldn't conceive of my dad, who never stopped moving and could hardly bear to wait in a line of any kind, stuck in a box. *He must hate this.*

Only he didn't, because he had ceased.

Or had gone elsewhere. His certainty never veered from what he was taught, which at times agitated me.

"But how can you not even question, Dad? How do you *know*?"

He gave me the smile, conveying that he loved me immensely and that what I'd just said was preposterous. "I just know." It really was that simple for him. I envied him that.

Sitting there, in the pew, I hoped he was right.

I also wondered in my Catholic way, outwardly accepting the faith's singular staunch narrative of the afterlife but inwardly entertaining otherworldly speculations, if he was somehow present.

I had ruffled my parents when, as a kid, I told them my friends and I had played with a Ouija board at a sleepover. They were equally disgruntled to learn that in my twenties, I had gone with friends to a psychic.

"It's just for fun," I protested with a laugh.

They frowned at me. "You shouldn't be messing with that stuff"—stuff including not only Ouija boards and psychics but also astrology, crystals, tarot cards, ghost hunting, or anything suggestive of a power of any kind deriving from any source other than God, in the strictest Catholic sense. Interest in this type of "hocus pocus, nonsense" indicated that a person had strayed too far and become susceptible to the darkness.

I had considered arguing the point that Catholics loved magic, though they didn't advertise it that way. They made pilgrimages to sites in France and Mexico and Israel where they believed miracles had occurred. They wore medallions depicting specific saints to help them travel safely or find lost items or stay sober. They believed that placing the body parts of saints in churches sanctified them. If they sensed evil in their homes, they called a priest to drive it out. I had always thought of Catholics as devoted practitioners of the magic they said they denounced.

It seemed possible that my dad had hung around to attend his funeral. I would have, given the choice. It seemed possible that death brought a comprehensive knowing, that he could now see all that he could not before, including the full scope of his daughter. It seemed possible that in death, he had at last learned of my affair.

Considering this, I felt what I had scarcely felt since Dutch and I began: guilt. Maybe I had disappointed my dad. And if, if I had—the prospect made me shrink, as small and ashamed as I had been in middle school when he caught me sneaking a twenty out of his wallet. I had always wanted to make him happy.

We can't wait for your wains. Over and over again he had said it. It would have made him happy. And now, he was gone.

I'm so sorry, Dad. I wanted to weep into his shoulder like I did as a penitent middle schooler, the press of my cheeks dampening the scratchy flannel. *I'm so sorry.*

The adult in me argued with the middle schooler. *Don't be sorry.* This shouldering of responsibility for another person's happiness was impossible. Absurd, really, that a grown woman would feel beholden to her parents, to such a dated imperative that didn't account at all for what she might want.

But I did want what you wanted.

I thought of baby Liam's baptism and how, once stripped of his ridiculously long, frilly white gown, he had been passed among the adults for them to admire. My dad took a turn holding the small, swaddled, powdery-smelling creature. I watched as Liam's tiny fingers escaped their blankets and seized my dad's thumb with surprising force. I watched as Liam contemplated my dad, who radiated in return.

So many adults gave their aging parents the joy his face registered then. Failure sat on my ribcage like a rock.

Dad died. I felt, though I was forty-four and sitting beside my mom, like an orphaned child. Maybe Dutch had felt this way his whole life.

Where is Dutch? I stole a backward glance at the packed church, past Tim, seated a few rows back, his face creased with sorrow and love. I scanned the back pews. Dutch was not there.

I shifted on the hard wooden pew and tried to focus on the readings and the homily. I blinked away the priest's flung droplets of holy water and clouds of incense, the unmistakable smell of death. I wished Catholic funerals were like other kinds, where the mourners wailed and clutched at their dead and fell to the ground.

Catholic funerals were as notably devoid of openly expressed sorrow as our weddings were of joy. Why did sorrow embarrass us? What was the collective instinct toward a decorous, buttoned-up version? Sniffling muffled into tissues. Discreet dabbing of eyes.

Only during "Be Not Afraid" and "On Eagle's Wings" did the grief well up and show itself. These songs named and assuaged our greatest fears. *Your loved one has not ceased or been cast alone into some unfathomable darkness. Your loved one has been received.*

These were also the songs included in every Catholic funeral that every Catholic had ever attended. When they began, people allowed themselves to weep for the deceased, but also for every other person they had ever grieved, and all the grief of all the mourners was bound and pressed together in these hymns, as pages in the hymnals.

When I returned to my pew after Communion, I scanned the back of the church again. Dutch was not there. When everyone stood for the final hymn, I looked one last time. He was not there. And when my mom and I, arm in arm, followed the coffin down the center aisle, the other mourners watched us, wiped their eyes, and thought they understood: shattering event, losing a spouse and a parent. But I saw the lie within the terrible depths and terrible shallows of my grief, the lie and shame in my weeping. It was for the man in the box being carried from the church, but it was also for the man missing from the back of it.

15

I *have high confidence in my understanding of Dutch's sober lifestyle, habits, and character.*

"I couldn't get away," Dutch later told me, his words slurring. "My wife had the flu."

If true, if he had not in fact panicked at the prospect of entering the church, if his own comfort had not in fact outweighed his feeling for me, what an entirely plausible reason not to come. The flu. My dad would have stayed with my mom. Tim would have stayed with me if I allowed it. It was a most acceptable and obvious course of action.

Because he is married. I forgot during our phone calls, when I was standing in his sunlight. Then, a sudden thrust into darkness, a shock each time. *He is married.*

I visited my mom almost daily, always wondering when I arrived whether I was crowding her, always wondering when I left if I was abandoning her. I kept asking, "Are you seeing people?"

"All the time." She reported that so-and-so had come by to do some household chore, that this one took her to lunch, that that one took her shopping. People's aid had an almost relentless quality, and her sisters' most of all. Instead of asking, they let themselves in and announced the task or errand they were bent on completing.

Two weeks after the funeral, I arrived at the house and found my mom in the bedroom, clutching the garish, stripy jersey my dad always wore to Gaelic Park. The rest of his clothes bulged from garbage bags, piled outside the abruptly half-empty closet.

I thought of Nan's sanctuary, every trace of her stripped from it after her death. "Aunt Peggy and Aunt Maeve?" I asked, gesturing at the bags.

"Yes, they were here," my mom said. "They're taking it to Goodwill. Which I suppose is a good idea."

She looked so alone, standing there holding the jersey, that I wanted to cry.

"Mom." I advanced. "You don't have to get rid of this stuff. At least not right now. Or, not all of it. Or any of it, if you don't want to. Do what you want." As soon as I said the words, I heard their clattering stupidity. Her wants had nothing to do with any of this.

"Well." She kneaded and twisted the jersey in her veined hands. "Maybe I'll just keep this one."

The following day, all the bags vanished.

Two months later, she and I were sitting at the kitchen table eating takeout directly from the cardboard cartons when she said, "Your dad and I used to talk about you, and the house."

I speared a piece of broccoli. "What about the house?"

"We wondered if you might want it when we're gone."

I chewed as I processed. I had never really considered the fate of the house because I had never really considered the death of my parents. These events had lurked so far in the distant, hazy future that they warranted no serious thought.

My mom gave up on her chopsticks with a frustrated sigh, left the table and returned with a fork. "Would you want the house one day?"

"I don't know." I looked around the kitchen I'd known my entire life. "Do I need to know? Right now?"

"No. Not right now."

"So I can think about it?"

"Absolutely."

We ate quietly for the next few minutes. I cleared our debris from the table, and a marked fatigue descended on my mom all at once, a new pattern since the funeral. She retreated to her bedroom for a nap.

I wandered where I wouldn't disturb her. In the living room, I surveyed the decades-old dark-green carpet and draperies, the floral print couch, the clawfoot oak curio cabinets. To access the small sunken family room adjacent to the kitchen, I took the single step down, which I had tripped on hundreds, maybe thousands of times. The den, even with all the lights on during the day, remained shadowy within the confines of its heavy wood paneling.

The house was as familiar to me as my reflection. But, inspecting it with the eyes of a potential owner, I saw how very dated it was. Though my parents had always done meticulous maintenance, the house had hardly changed in my lifetime.

Could I live here? I tried to imagine it, moving around the house alone, my parents both gone. They had animated the house with their endless visitors, their parties and holidays, the hum of daily life, their marriage. Could I do the same with my friends coming and going, my books on the shelves, my art on the walls? Could I do it with my bedding and dishes, my movies and music, my noise?

I could picture only the stillness, sitting in it, surrounded by artifacts from all our former lives as an intact family. The thought was unimaginably sad. Without my parents in it, the home I had always loved would become a monument to loss.

Or, I thought, maybe it would feel like Tim's house, waiting for a family and a life to fill it up. With only me, our house would never feel full.

My mom and I dragged ourselves through the holidays, sharing the hope that some small relief might come if we could survive until January 2. We hosted nothing but attended everything and smiled to make other people feel better. We put up the Christmas tree and cried through the whole process. We left the wreaths, stockings, garlands, nativity set, and Christmas village in their basement boxes, alongside my dad's outside lights. We left the tree standing through January, forlorn and unlit.

When I finally, gently told her in March that I didn't want the house, I worried my decision would hurt her. I expected her to protest and try to change my mind. Instead she said, "I might sell then. I've been thinking about it."

This hadn't even occurred to me. I couldn't imagine her living anywhere else. "Where would you go?"

"I'm not sure. I'm just thinking about it. But Maeve and Peggy have brought up some good points."

I frowned. "Such as?"

"Well." She kept her gaze on the laundry spread across her bed, waiting to be folded. "Such as, maybe this is too much house for one person. Maybe it's too much work, too much money."

"Mom." I moved some towels out of the way and sat down on the bed. "This is your house. This is *our* house. It's never been too much house before."

"I know. But things are a little different now."

This truth occupied us for a quiet moment.

I helped her fold. "The house is paid for, right?"

"It is." She shook some wrinkles from a sheet.

"And you've been friends with all your neighbors for years. And they'll be taking care of the outside stuff. You won't have to do any of it."

After the funeral, the neighbors had overwhelmed us with their generosity, lining up to take charge of the lawn mowing, leaf raking, snow shoveling.

"But if I moved to a condo, I wouldn't need anyone to do all that extra work. Maeve and Peggy told me about some nice ones right by them," she continued. "And the real-estate agent said this house would sell fast. She said tons of young couples and families want to get into this neighborhood."

"You've already talked to an *agent?* Jesus, Mom."

She shot me a sharp look.

"I'm sorry. But, Mom, if you've already talked to an agent, you're not just thinking about it."

"I am. I'm just getting information. And I told my sisters that I wouldn't be ready to make any decisions until I knew if you wanted the house, and then maybe I still wouldn't be ready. These are big decisions. They understand."

I snorted. "I bet they do."

She sagged. "They're trying to help."

"They bludgeon you with their help."

On the phone with Dutch that night, I told him, "My aunts will be coming for me any time now."

"How do you know?"

I rubbed my face. "I just know."

In the immediate aftermath of my dad's death, my aunts and I had managed to orbit my mom without crashing into one another. Soon enough, the tension returned. They always seemed either dissatisfied with the amount of care I gave my mom, or irritated when they showed up at the house and found me there.

After church on Easter, the family descended on Aunt Peggy's house. The dining room table was draped in white linen, adorned with a large Lenox vase of tulips and loaded with food. The adults inside took any available spot, trying to sip their drinks without upsetting the plates balanced on their knees. I joined the group that headed outside to watch the kids, who scrambled around the large yard in their suits and poufy dresses, looking for plastic, pastel, candy-filled eggs.

From the sound of it, my cousin Patrick had revealed that he had a girlfriend in his first-grade class. This information elicited from his young cousins a chorus of "ooohs," kissing noises, and the enduring chant: *First comes love, then comes marriage. Then comes baby in a baby carriage.*

I considered intervening on Patrick's behalf. But just as quickly as they turned on him, they tired of their taunts and returned to their egg hunt. I slipped around the side of the house to the driveway and lit a cigarette.

Two minutes later my aunts emerged from the house and cornered me.

"We've been wanting to talk to you about your mom," Aunt Peggy began, lighting a cigarette of her own. "But not in front of her."

"She has so much on her *plate*," Aunt Maeve said, standing at a distance from our smoke, her nose wrinkled with distaste. "We should probably keep this conversation between *us*."

I fought the temptation to light five cigarettes and shove them all into my mouth at once. "Are we talking about the house?"

"We want to make sure you don't want it."

"I don't want it." I exhaled. "I told my mom that."

"That's *good*," Aunt Maeve said quickly. "I'm sure you agree that she doesn't need all that *space*."

"No single woman does. It's just too much," Aunt Peggy explained.

"Aunt Peggy." I gestured at her house. "You stayed here after Uncle Sean died. It wasn't too much for you."

"That's different."

"How is that different?"

"I have five kids and seventeen grandkids who are in and out of here all the time," she huffed. "This house is a second home for all of them."

"So our house isn't worth keeping because there are fewer of us?"

"It's not *your* house. It's your mom's house."

"And with her just having *you*," Aunt Maeve jumped in, "and your situation being what it *is*…"

"Now, if you had a family of your own—"

"We could see how you might feel differently."

"But since you're on your own, and your mom is now too," Aunt Peggy finished, "I'm sure you agree that we should all be thinking about what's best for her."

"*We* should?"

"Yes, of course." They looked impatient.

"I'm not sure *we* should be thinking about what's best for her. I think she can decide that for herself."

I saw how this suggestion riled Aunt Peggy. "You have to understand your mom."

My voice went cold. "I understand my mom."

"You don't understand her frame of mind right now," Aunt Peggy snapped. "She's not thinking of herself, she's thinking of you. She feels obligated to stay in the house for you."

"But if you encourage her to *sell*," Aunt Maeve interjected. "If she knows she has your *blessing*—"

"Then she'll feel free to do what she wants," Aunt Peggy concluded. "You have to be fair to her and not make this about you."

I looked at my aunts, arms folded across their chests, so intent on shepherding their widowed sister. They forgot that I'd lost someone too.

"I want my mom to do what she wants, but I think she might need more time to figure that out," I said. "She might *want* to stay in the house. She's been happy there for a long time."

Is she still? Could she be again? I shook away these questions and resolved to return to them later. I tried to draw myself up before my aunts, making myself taller, and force the hot flush from my cheeks.

For years my dad had weathered his sisters-in-law's intrusions with good-natured eye rolls and head shakes. When they were on what he called "one of their tears," he had leaned toward me with a conspiratorial smile, gestured at them, and dropped his voice. "Ya know, they'll go through ya for a shortcut."

As they frowned at me, hands on their ample hips, I felt as I always had in their presence. I was still a bumbling child, perpetually either about to do or having just done something wrong.

I had also robbed them of their heirloom. I saw how they eyed my ring, the ring they believed was their mother's. They'd never forgiven me.

Aunt Peggy dropped her cigarette, ground it out with her shoe, and bent to pick up the butt. As she stood, she sniffed, "We just don't want your mom guilted into staying in the house."

"And I don't want her bullied into leaving."

The air between us froze.

Inside, Aunt Peggy's house teemed with families. I hovered

alone. *If you had a family of your own.* I considered going home and wondered if I could pull it off without upsetting my mom.

Patrick approached to show off his spoils from the egg hunt. "Look how much candy I got," he crowed, thrusting his basket toward me. I peered into it as he studied me. "Are you sad?"

"A little," I admitted.

"Because grown-ups don't get candy?" He was full of sympathy.

"That's right."

He dug around in his basket, presenting me with a handful, and said, "Tell my mom and dad I shared, okay?"

"I promise I will."

Off he ran.

At home that night, still in my dress, I lay on my couch changing channels and replaying the exchange with my aunts. They thought I was being selfish.

Am I? I picked bits of tin foil off the chocolate footballs Patrick had given me. I wanted to hang on to my sense of home a little while longer. I wanted to postpone another loss. But maybe, just as I couldn't imagine myself in our house without my family, my mom couldn't either.

I had considered myself her advocate. I wondered now if I was just one more person pushing her around.

I thought of Dutch, in Florida with his family. The certainty of my phone's silence that night, and for the next week, brought with it a wave of loneliness.

On his trips, did he ever stand on the sand, gaze out at the ocean, and think of me? What was he doing right now with his family? Maybe, away from home, they abandoned the formalities of the holiday and opted instead for the beach. Maybe, in search of brunch, they located a restaurant with ice sculptures and an omelet station and a mute employee in an Easter bunny costume. What, I wondered, did Dutch's daughter know of the Easter bunny?

He would tell me all these things when he returned. But for now, only the silence. We never talked on holidays. *Because he is married.*

Other facts of our relationship blinked at me. One was that no matter what existed between us, his and his wife's intimacy was a kind that only came with shared day-to-day life. She probably knew the balance of their joint checking account. She probably kept in mind his particular likes and dislikes when grocery shopping. She probably expected that he would tend to her when she had the flu.

Another was that no matter how much he called me, no matter how much space I occupied in his thoughts, I occupied none at all in his real life.

I thought of how Johnny Cash had died just four months after June Carter. Many believed he couldn't bear to be in a world without June and died of a broken heart. Surely if he had died first, June would have followed as quickly.

When I met Dutch, I had been sure I would never feel alone again. It seemed impossible with this person in the world, even in his absences, because he always somehow lingered nearby and always eventually returned. But what if this person were suddenly, simply gone?

This fear had always surfaced where Dutch was concerned but intensified after my dad died. Dutch had always lived near some unnamed danger. And if it took him, no one in his life would even know to tell me. He would just disappear. For good.

I asked him, "Does anyone know about me?"

He said no. Of course he said no. The word was so small and serrated.

To a few people in his life, I was a faint, misty figure from his distant past. To most of them, I didn't exist at all. I longed for him to say my name, out loud, to someone.

I needed someone, somewhere, beyond the isolation of my island, to bear witness. I needed, if only with Claire and Fiona, if only during one conversation with each of them, to align my interior and exterior lives.

16

I started with Claire, at breakfast in a diner. When I finished my story, she sipped her coffee. "He's been married, what, two years?"

"About."

She nodded a little. "He didn't get very far, did he." It was a statement. Then, "I can't really picture you as a mistress."

"Mistress," I repeated, trying it out. "That's a funny word. It's so…"

"Demeaning?"

I guffawed in spite of myself. "I was going to say old-fashioned."

"Lover? Side chick?"

"Gross."

"The other woman?"

"She's the other woman."

Claire arched an eyebrow. "She probably wouldn't see it that way."

"I know." I could think of a dozen names for what I was, names other women would whisper and spit. Women like me were as reviled as pedophiles.

Claire asked, "Does it matter anyway? What you call it?"

It didn't.

On some level, the entire affair was preposterous, my position laughable. The exceptions I made and had always made for Dutch, I couldn't conceive of in any other context.

I wanted to be noble. I wanted to construct thick, resolute black lines all around myself. And still, my lines never helped when Dutch advanced. They always slipped out of place and collapsed.

I gazed across the table at Claire, who shifted in her seat. "I feel like you want me to say something."

"I do."

"What do you want me to say?"

"I don't know. Anything. Please."

She took a bite of omelet, thinking. "It happens all the time."

"What does?"

"This." She swallowed. "People get unhappy. Or bored. Or they want to feel attractive again. Or who knows."

I pushed my eggs around my plate, feeling my air seeping from a dozen tiny punctures. "That's pretty reductive, isn't it?"

"Is it? I mean, you guys sit on the phone at night, right? Once the wife goes to bed and he's rattling around that giant house by himself?"

"Yeah."

"So don't you ever wonder if he just wants *someone* to talk to, and that maybe this isn't specifically about you?"

"It *feels* pretty specific to me." Sometimes I knew what Dutch and I shared. Sometimes I feared that I was a distraction from his loneliness and boredom, a passport to his lost youth, a fantasy he could enter and exit at will.

"I guess anything's possible," I mumbled, my deflation complete.

"I'm not trying to hurt you. I'm just saying that when people aren't getting what they need in a relationship, they find it somewhere else. They dig up some old flame, they start flirting with someone at work." A shadow flashed across her face. "Happens all the time."

I had come to breakfast prepared for dismay, anger maybe, but not for a dismissive shrug. Now that I had revealed my secret, shimmering treasure, it had been unceremoniously cast into a bargain bin.

"Claire."

"What?"

"Not every"—I dropped my voice—"not every affair is just a symptom of an unhappy relationship. I know that's common wisdom, but people have affairs for other reasons."

"Such as?"

I felt a rising in my throat, an opportunity. With exactly the right words, I could show her that Dutch and I could not be reduced to some lurid cliché. I could show her that we were something different, something entirely outside the realm of what other people were.

The opportunity passed. I opened my hands, flattened them on the table, and said, "Love."

Claire was silent. Then, "Remember Julian?"

I had never met him. No one had. When their brief relationship ended, Claire retreated as she always did and said little when she reemerged. But there they were, wounds that showed, raw and gleaming. I couldn't remember seeing Claire so vulnerable.

I was careful to use the past tense. "You really liked him."

Claire sipped her coffee. "He was married." I gaped at her. She continued, "I didn't know that when we got together. He didn't wear his ring. He didn't have any pictures in his office."

"You never went to his house?"

"He said it was being renovated. We always went out or to my house."

I was thunderstruck. "How did you find out?"

"He told me. You know, eventually." She spoke over the rim of her coffee cup.

"Claire." I shook my head. "Why didn't you tell me that's why you broke up?"

"Uh..." She tried to laugh. "Because that's not why we broke up. Or when."

I let this sink in. Then, "Just tell me. Tell me what happened."

She said that when he told her the truth, she was devastated. Furious. Stunned. The possibility that he might be married had never even occurred to her. She said that she didn't end it then because she wanted him so much. She said that ultimately, he ended it, telling her he'd had fun but needed to work it out with his wife.

Since then, she said, work had been agony. They crossed paths every day. When they passed each other in the hallways and sat in the same meetings, she said he looked right past and through her like a ghost. He'd been inside her, told her he loved her. "Now, it's like we never even met."

Also, her co-workers knew. She said she didn't know how they knew, but the change in the air was as distinct as the smell of rotting food. She heard it in the innuendos and saw it in the leering. When her male colleagues gathered in one of their offices and saw her coming, they lowered their voices and closed the door. Then she heard a burst of laughter from inside.

She had always felt her sex so conspicuously in this sea of men. She had tried to make herself sexless by working harder than any of them, by not only matching but surpassing them. She had made herself inscrutable.

"And now, everything I've accomplished, all the work I've put in, every little scrap of respect I had to fight for…" Claire fluttered her fingers through the air, dust swirling away in a breeze.

I wanted to climb across the table and wrap my arms around her. This glimpse of my knight out of her armor disconcerted me, like seeing a normally fluffy dog that had just been shaved.

"I thought we had what everyone's looking for," Claire said. "But in the end, I was the only one who thought that."

With Dutch, this was my greatest fear.

When I reached for her hands, she returned a quick pat. Then, her usual briskness restored, she drew her hands beneath the table. She said, when I asked her, that no one else knew.

"But why didn't you tell us while this was all happening?"

"You and Dutch have been talking for a year. Why didn't you tell me until now?"

We faced each other across the table. Perhaps these betrayals and secrecies were the benign kind, if such a kind existed. But here they were, suddenly showing and raw and gleaming, in the middle of our sisterhood.

Claire said, "You better be careful. This could get bad."

"I know."

Claire said, "You could open your door one day and find a

bunch of people standing there with pitchforks and torches and shit like that."

"I know. Prada pitchforks."

Claire said, "Please don't tell Fi about me."

"I won't."

She set down her fork and wiped her mouth. "Are you going to tell her about Dutch?"

I turned the question around and around in my mind, like the sapphire on my finger.

If a person could be shown her friend's ugliest truth and love her anyway, if such a person existed, it was Fiona. If a person existed with whom I could find the right words, it was Fiona. She had always understood me in a way that other people did not.

But family was Fiona's church, and she was a true believer. Her husband and children were her sacraments. So maybe the words wouldn't matter at all. Maybe they could only ever be the words of a heretic, revealing not the strength of my connection to Dutch but the weakness of our character. Not a sacred union, but a desecration.

Maybe my affair was the one disclosure Fiona could not be asked to absorb.

Dutch said, "I need a favor."

"What is it?" I couldn't imagine. I frequently needed lifelines: loans when my old Honda broke down, friends' help painting walls and moving furniture, extensions and payment plans for bills that my salary couldn't absorb. Dutch had so much money that he never needed to ask anything of anyone. But he needed this, a letter, and he couldn't buy it.

After years of putting it off, he said he wanted to try to get his driver's license reinstated. "I talked to a lawyer, just to find out what's involved. It would be a pain in the ass."

"But worth it."

"Probably worth it. This license issue is the last thing still—"

He exhaled. "Still tying me to all that. I want it gone."

The lawyer had told him that, to move through the process, he'd need a collection of character witness letters. *Just like the ones you needed years ago to get your probation terminated.* "And you want me to write one?"

"Would you?"

"Can't your wife do it?"

"She is, and so are a bunch of other people. But I need more, and they're supposed to be from people who've known me a long time."

Fifteen years.

"Okay." I swallowed. "What do I have to say?"

He told me he would email me the court's instructions.

I had in the past written somewhat disingenuously, for instance in grad school courses that called for endless literary analyses. Unsure of how they should sound or even the point of such an endeavor, I wrote them with sweeping, grandiose urgency that suggested that the very fate of literature depended on my interpretation of it. Thinking of them now made me cringe.

I had also found myself in the uncomfortable position of writing recommendation letters for students who aggravated and fatigued me. One such student, a pit bull named Teresa, interrupted lectures with her barking questions, challenged the merit of every lesson, monopolized office hours, and harangued me whenever she got an A- instead of an A.

When she cornered me to ask for a recommendation letter for her law school application, I was so flustered that I agreed. When I sat down to the grim task, I wanted to pronounce Teresa a giant pain in the ass. Instead, I wrote, "Her tenacity and passion for argument suggest that she is well suited to the study of law." This statement, I rationalized at the time, was at least somewhat true.

But this letter for Dutch was different. To serve its purpose, I needed to tell a number of outright lies.

Toying with my ring, the pad of my thumb finding and turning the warm circle, I opened the email and reviewed the court's instructions. They said my letter should describe the nature and duration of my relationship with Dutch, my familiarity with his case. They wanted to know what I knew.

I know everything. Someone got hurt. Someone besides me.

They wanted to know my history with Dutch. They wanted details about our current relationship, including the activities we engaged in and the general content of our communications.

Most of all, they wanted to know about his sobriety.

Dutch's lawyer had advised him, "The people writing your letters should be clear that they have frequent, face-to-face interactions with you. This will carry more weight than saying they only see you once in a while or only talk to you on the phone."

Dutch relayed this to me. Then he added, "Just remember this letter's for court." I heard the trepidation in his pause. "So, you know."

I knew what he meant. Keep it short. He was no doubt thinking of all those letters I'd sent him years earlier, all those filled pages of stationery, thick and folded into red envelopes.

Where Dutch was concerned, I had never been able to keep it short.

But this time, I resolved to try. I pulled out my laptop and tapped the keys.

Fiona and I sat side by side on her deck, barefoot with beers in hand, as Denny wrangled Liam and Maggie to bed. Through an open window I could hear their protests. The backyard was dotted with soccer balls and dominated by a hulking, primary-colored plastic playhouse.

Fiona asked about my mom. I asked about her plan for the summer. "Do you and Denny get a break now that school's out?"

I expected her to say that summer afforded them a brief reprieve from the frenetic juggling of their students' and their own kids' needs. Then I laughed a little as she started talking, remembering who she was. When part of her schedule opened, she promptly filled it up again.

She told me that while Denny was helping a buddy with construction for the summer, she would be Liam and Maggie's chauffeur, carting them between countless practices, games, and day camps. "I'm basically going to be living in my car." She had agreed to watch some of the neighbors' kids too. "Might as well. With mine running around, what's a few more?" The director of their church's summer program for kids had asked her to help out, and she thought she could probably manage it.

She and Denny were also planning and saving for a trip to Disney World, she continued. They needed to call a plumber. They'd probably refinish their deck. They had resolved to spend more time with their parents, who complained that they didn't get enough time with the grandkids.

I looked at her in wonder. Fiona had not done what so many people did when they started families and discovered the rapid evaporation of time. She had not faded from her friends' lives, reappearing only occasionally as a novelty. On that evening, as if by magic, she had conjured time for me when there simply was none.

She and Denny had just seen Tim, Fiona told me. "The other night, when you were under the weather."

I nodded, my tone vague. "That's right. How'd it go?"

"That's the thing." Fiona glanced over at me. "I need to talk to you."

She knows. For a fleeting, panicked second, I thought Claire had let my secret slip.

Fiona continued, "I need to talk to you about Tim."

"Oh." I felt a wave of relief, then puzzlement. "Okay. What about him?"

"Well." Fiona sipped her beer. "When he was here, he got to talking. About you."

Inwardly I flinched. "Go ahead."

"He has this theory."

Picturing him theorizing about me to my friends, I groaned.

"Want to hear it?"

"Not really."

"He thinks you're dragging your feet with him because you've been hurt. He thinks you just need more time."

She waited for me to say something. When I didn't, she sipped again, suddenly tense. "So I want to know what you're going to do about him."

I also took a sip. "I'm not sure I understand the question."

Fiona's voice was even. "Yes, you do."

I did. I just didn't want to recount the conversations Tim had been initiating with increasing frequency, conversations loaded with implications.

Fiona did it for me. "He asks you these questions, trying to figure out where you're coming from, where he stands with you."

"Sometimes. So?"

"So he has the right to ask these questions."

"The right?" I flared a little. "I'm not sure that's the 'right' word. Forgive the pun."

"It is the right word. He deserves to understand the situation. And you always come back with some bullshit."

I relied on a stock set of responses to his probing: I had a lot going on. I didn't know. I didn't want to be pushed. I would probably change careers. I was figuring it all out. But after decades of friendship, I was flabbergasted to find myself in this moment with Fiona, poised for what felt like our first real fight.

"And when he can't get a straight answer out of you, he tells you what he wants. I know he's talked to you about this." Fiona paused to see if I'd challenge her, and when I didn't, she pressed on. "He's hinted around a thousand times at getting a new job where he doesn't have to travel anymore, and you never even say anything when he brings it up. You just come back with more bullshit about how he should do what's best for his career."

"He should. He's a grown man. He has to figure that out for himself." Fiona cocked her head at me.

"I'm not going to tell him what to do with his career, Fiona. It has nothing to do with me."

"It has everything to do with you. He's not asking for career advice. He's asking if you want him around more, if that would change the situation. He would quit in a second if you said you wanted him to."

"I *don't* want him to. I don't want him to do anything." My voice rose. My stomach hurt. I felt a hot, surprising rush of anger toward Tim.

He's such a good guy. Everyone who told me that was right. And because he was such a good guy, because I allowed the relationship to begin and hadn't allowed it to advance, I was the villain. I had always felt this full responsibility. Now I considered the possibility that he shared some.

I wondered if Claire's theory about Dutch wanting *someone*, maybe not necessarily, precisely me, had some traction after all. I wondered suddenly if it applied to Tim.

The future he talked about never sounded like a specific vision for his happiness with a specific person. It sounded instead like a script that needed only some cast members' names filled in.

My beer bottle rattled in my hands. "Jesus, Fiona."

"What?"

"Did you know he has a whole family of bikes hanging on his garage wall?"

"So he's a planner. He knows what he wants. So?"

"So walking into that house is like walking onto a set. And he's got this role to fill, and it feels like you and Tim and everyone else got together and assigned it to me when I wasn't there." I had hidden entire parts of myself from him. Maybe they were inconsequential. "Everyone seems to think I owe him something."

"You do."

"What exactly do I owe him?"

"You owe it to him to try. Work on this relationship if you want to be in it. Make an effort."

I rubbed my face. "This relationship is all effort."

"Then be decent and let him go if you don't want him." Fiona's voice rose too. "At least do that. He's a good guy. He deserves to be happy."

"Do I?"

"Do you think you're capable?"

"What does *that* mean?"

"I just don't understand you. I know you want to share your life with someone. I know you do. But you spent your thirties waiting around for something that was never going to happen." This unprompted reference to Dutch flustered me even more. "I think you really thought that one day, he'd wake up and magically be different. Everything would magically be different. You're so smart. Why couldn't you see that that was *never* going to happen?"

Acid curled its way up to my throat.

"And for someone who loves to wave her feminist flag—"

"Okay." I slammed my bottle down. "Stop."

"That's always been so big with you. You said you understood your worth. You said you believed in feminism."

"I did. I do."

"But the whole time you were talking about what you believed, you were lying down in traffic for a guy that treated you like shit. You did that for ten *years*."

Fifteen.

"And for the last three years, Tim's been right in front of you, trying to make you happy. He wants to give you a life. He's *right* here. Why won't you take it?"

Because I can't love him. It was the one thing I could say that was a whole truth, not morally compromised, and as unalterable as my DNA.

Instead, I returned fire. "I *have* a life. I don't need it to look like yours. You don't think anyone can be happy unless their life looks exactly like yours."

"You're happy?" Fiona gestured at me. "Like this?"

"Like what, Fiona?"

"Don't tell me you're happy. And don't tell me you're a feminist. I don't think you're either one. Actually, I think you're—"

A fraud.

She stopped herself. I stood. So did she.

"And anyway, let's forget *your* happiness for a minute. Let's put that to the side. I mean"—Fiona's volume drew Denny to the closed glass doors, his face a question mark—"do you ever think about Tim? About how much of his time you've wasted? Do you even realize how many women would love to love him?"

My inner voice leveled these charges all the time. The shock was hearing them out loud from Fiona.

Seeing Denny, remembering the kids, I bit my lip and forced back tears, like a middle-school girl whose closest girlfriends were suddenly, publicly turning on her.

My voice trembled. "What's happening right now? Where's my friend?"

In her silence and level gaze, another revelation. I wasn't having this fight with my friend Fiona. I was having it with Tim's friend Fiona.

And of course that was the case. I'd been a constant in her life, but so too now had Tim, who was no longer just some tangent of her husband's. After all of Fiona and Denny's parties, he was the one who stayed late to help clean up. He was the one who sat on the living room floor letting Liam and Maggie scale him, who pushed them on their swings, who kicked the ball around the yard with them. He was the one at their dinner table, talking about his life, about me, when I had invented some reason not to be there.

I shook all over as I drove home. I had agonized over what I could ask Fiona to withstand for the sake of our friendship. I hadn't realized she would make that decision.

17

Dear Sir or Madam:

I am writing on behalf of Dutch Van Lokeren, whom I've known for fifteen years. We met when we were twenty-nine.

Dutch and I dated for four years. Early on in our relationship, he shared with me the details of his legal history. He also expressed deep remorse for his actions and for their negative impact on all involved.

Dutch told me that he had been committed to his sobriety since the time of the accident. Drugs and alcohol were not part of our interactions, and at no point did I observe him using either.

After four years, we ended our romantic relationship. This decision was mutual, amicable, and unrelated to drugs or alcohol. Since dating, Dutch and I have maintained platonic contact. We communicate regularly, and I find great value in our ongoing friendship.

Presently, we have lunch on a monthly basis, where we talk primarily about family. Drugs and alcohol have no role in this shared time. It is clear to me that now, at forty-four, Dutch is a much different man than he was at twenty-one. Now, his wife, his daughter, and his sobriety are the center of his life.

I have high confidence in my understanding of Dutch's sober lifestyle, habits, and character. If you would like to speak further, please feel free to contact me. I am happy to provide any other information you may need.

Thank you for your time.

I turned Dutch's letter in my hands. No midnight ink this time. No heavy cream stationery or red envelope. A hopelessly bland-looking document, 12-point font, Times New Roman, generic black ink, 8½ x11" white printer paper.

The stranger who notarized it would see only another brief business letter, not a love letter, the best one I'd ever written. And now, Dutch had to collect it.

We would finally face each other.

At the end of *Walk the Line*, Johnny Cash and June Carter finally united. No longer did other people stand between them. No longer did addiction stand between them. There was no more line. He lifted her in the air and kissed her.

Dutch asked me to mail the letter to his attorney's office.

He got his license reinstated, his victory. I heard his exhilaration when he called me with the news. He was walking out of the courthouse, he said, then running home to pack and hitting the road. The three-day trip to his hometown would include a golf outing with some high school buddies, a visit to his mom, and a detour to see Jimmy. The name made my heart sink.

The next evening, I was reading on my apartment balcony when a sleek black BMW glided up and halted, like a delivery person double-checking an address. I watched it take a tentative turn into the driveway. No one I knew had a car this nice.

As soon as the well-dressed blond emerged from the car, I recognized her. At the same instant, my phone chimed. I almost ignored it, since the air all around me seemed to be filling with shattering glass, but Tim had never sent me a text in all caps before.

My gaze skimmed it. WE NEED TO TALK. And all at once, the chaotic blur before me slid into perfect focus.

I could picture Dutch returning home from court the day before. He would have had a file or an envelope containing his paperwork and notarized letters, including mine. He was giddy, rushing. I could picture him tossing the file somewhere careless, maybe on the dining room table, before throwing some clothes in a bag and hurrying out the door.

His wife would have noticed the file and been curious, would have opened it and leafed through its contents. Almost all the names at the bottom of these notarized letters would have been familiar and predictable, names of men she and Dutch saw all the time, men who came to their parties and invited them to their own. But she would have seen one surprising name, mine. Maybe she had remembered it from her wedding guest list.

Strange, a wife would have thought if reading this letter, that her husband had never said a word about me, though my letter attested to years of regular contact with him. Strange, a wife would have thought, tucking the letters back into the file, that her husband was intimate enough with me to ask me to write such a thing.

Googling me would have been an obvious and immediate decision. But with Dutch out of town, she would have had the liberty to conduct a more rigorous investigation. Maybe she found and read an old stack of handwritten letters in red envelopes. Maybe she examined Dutch's phone bills. It probably wouldn't have occurred to her to look at them, until now. He paid the bills.

And if she looked at the phone bills, she would have found the hundreds of calls and thousands of texts Dutch had deleted from his history. They would all be there, page after page.

In the last year she must have known something was wrong. Uneasiness must have whispered inside her. When it did, she must have shaken her head and covered her ears. But if she had scrolled through this neat and lengthy list of undeniable betrayals, all the light would have drained away in an instant. She would have been knocked suddenly and violently into abject darkness.

She would have written a brief letter of her own, a message to someone named Tim on Facebook who appeared to be my boyfriend. And she wouldn't have had to search for my address. It was right there in my letter, per the court's instructions, along with my phone number and email.

Since the affair began, this exact scenario had played out in my head, thousands of times, filling me with horror and scrambling panic. Now that it was actually happening, calm descended on me. I set my book down and walked through my apartment, down the stairs, out the front door. I twisted the sapphire on my finger and heard the click of a car door closing. I approached the unfathomable figure, and we faced each other.

When I spoke, the quiet evenness of my voice surprised me. "I loved him first."

❧

My mom decided to sell the house. Her agent, an aggressively cheerful woman named Sandy, advised us on her walk-through, "Do what you can here before I list. *Such* a great neighborhood. This house is going to be *snatched* up."

We began preparing the house for a parade of strangers, sorting its contents room by room to determine what should be given away, what should be thrown away, and what should accompany my mom to her new condo, a tidy, sterile place full of divorcees and widows, down the street from Aunt Peggy and Aunt Maeve.

They helped my mom pack. I ran boxes to Goodwill. They worked in one room. I worked in another. We mastered the art of avoiding each other in the small house.

My mom said, "I don't feel like I'm moving. It doesn't feel real."

It felt instead like endless practice for an event that wouldn't actually happen. Throughout the process my mom stopped to ponder, at length, about whether to keep an item: a dainty teacup and saucer, so prettily hand painted but not part of a set, a bit of fabric she had intended to use but forgotten about, my dad's tools.

"I should probably have some tools at the condo, don't you think?"

"I think they should go to Dad's brothers." I was getting impatient. "Let's keep going."

But I also derailed our progress, calling out when I came across photo albums or my old ballet slippers or my dad's high-school yearbook, "Mom, come look at this!"

We stopped mid-project to gaze side by side at our discoveries, remembering. Then, realizing how long we'd been sitting, we hurried back to the task at hand.

Then one day, we wandered the house in search of more

work and found remarkably little left to do. Together we cleaned it top to bottom. A neighbor fixed a leaky faucet. I carried a ladder into my bedroom to scrape the stars off the ceiling. My mom hunted behind furniture for scuff marks on the walls.

Sandy walked through one more time and pronounced the house ready. Her assistant drove the For Sale sign into the lawn like a stake.

My mom asked Sandy if she thought we should do any paint touch-ups. I was hovering in the doorway with the record of my childhood growth. My fingers moved over the pencil markings and drew Sandy's attention.

"I wouldn't worry about these small imperfections," she said, squinting at the marks. "The buyers will want a project. I'm sure they'll repaint everything."

And then, it was over, the house snatched up, just as Sandy had said. As my mom and I pulled out of the driveway for the last time, she said, sitting shotgun, "I feel like we're coming back tonight, like I'm going to make dinner, like everything's the same."

So did I.

She looked out the window. "But it isn't, is it?"

No.

She said, "I hope the buyers don't rip out our trees."

The trees in the backyard, she meant, braided like my parents, the ones they considered separating and decided to leave intact.

Our trees. Her language of plurality flowed unhindered.

Once reasonably settled in at her new condo, she hugged me. I turned to leave, and she caught me by the arm. "When you come back, bring Tim."

Like almost everyone, she loved him. I didn't have the heart to tell her.

Claire asked afterward, "Do you want to drive by and scope out the new owners?"

"No. Too sad." I meant it when I said it. But I did drive

by a few weeks later, unable to stop myself, my steering wheel guiding the car as if of its own accord, onto my old street.

Pickup trucks lined it. Construction workers moved in and out of the house. On the front lawn sat a couple, the ambitious renovators Sandy had predicted, their plans already underway. Amidst the noise and activity of hammers and saws, they coaxed a tiny diapered girl on the grass to toddle between them.

I pictured them replacing carpet with hardwood and Formica countertops with granite, hanging a barn door, knocking down walls for an open concept. *This is theirs now.*

We had stripped away as much of ourselves as we could. Now they would erase the rest.

I kept my head down. I only went out if absolutely necessary. On this night, the need for tampons and toilet paper forced me into my car.

Standing in line at the drugstore, I heard my name. Instantly I felt sick. Before I could fully turn, someone was pulling me into a hug.

"Hey, Glick." Once extracted, I readjusted my arms around my tampons and unwieldy toilet paper. "Been a while."

"Yeah, I haven't seen you since the wedding." He cocked his head at me. "You a little under the weather?"

As ghastly as I looked in my dim apartment, I couldn't imagine how much worse it was under these fluorescent lights. "A little."

"How's the teaching gig?"

Dutch's wife had shown much more acuity than he had ever given her credit for or let on. In her research she had identified a friend of a friend as a member of my employer's Board of Directors. Using this channel and her impressive reach, she had conveyed information about me that she thought they ought to know.

When the firing squad summoned me, I hadn't even known why we were meeting. My confusion persisted when they produced a document, one of many in a large stack, from my hiring process years earlier. A code of conduct, they reminded me as they slid it across the table toward me, in which I had pledged "not to engage in any activities which reflected unfavorably upon the institution."

Then I remembered scrawling my name at the bottom of it. I had needed a job. I would have signed anything. Afterward, I had told Claire about it, and we had laughed together.

"This is my personal life. I haven't broken any laws." I had stared at them, dumbfounded. "Can—can you do this?"

They had stared back at me. They were a private Catholic university. They could do anything they wanted.

"Teaching's fine," I lied to Glick. "What've you been up to?"

"Same old." He smiled, jostling me. "But I hear you've been up to all *kinds* of things."

He loved a scandal. He wanted details. When I just shrugged, he looked disappointed.

Almost immediately, though, he brightened. "I guess Dutch probably told you about his latest adventure."

"No."

"You're kidding. He just told me the craziest story. You know his buddy Jimmy?"

I dropped my tampons. "I know of him."

"Right." He picked up the box, examined it, and handed it back to me. "So Dutch goes to see this guy and they end up back at Jimmy's house, which I guess is kind of a shithole. Plus all these people are there and they're creeping Dutch out. He said the whole scene is pretty sketchy. But he's waiting on Jimmy for something, I don't know what. And he ends up waiting around for, like, a while." Glick was animated. "So finally Dutch gets what he needs and takes off. And turns out, *right* after he leaves, Jimmy's house gets *raided*." Glick was practically crowing. "I guess the cops were watching the place for months. They took everyone who was there."

The clerk waved me toward the register. I paid as fast as I could.

"Talk about dodging a fucking bullet," Glick continued as he walked me to my car. "I can't believe he didn't tell you."

I dug around in my purse for my keys.

Glick shook his head with obvious admiration. "That guy. Always something, right?"

Always a next time.

I opened my car door. Glick leaned in for another hug. "All right. Well." He gestured at my face. "Take care of that. Feel better."

Off he trotted, visibly pleased to have relayed one splashy story to the subject of another.

All the way home, I cursed myself for having gone out. *That's what you get.* Once I'd sealed myself back inside my apartment, I dropped onto the couch. My hands shook. I could visualize the scene.

Dutch would have wanted a quick transaction. Maybe what he had wanted wasn't ready, or wasn't there yet, or maybe other matters had needed Jimmy's attention first. I could see Dutch moving further into the house, reluctant, irked by the wait. He was not accustomed to waiting.

A shithole, Glick had said. I imagined a ramshackle house that only got worse inside: smoke-yellowed walls, sparse, shabby furniture, overflowing ashtrays and bottles crowding every surface. A house like this would have repelled Dutch, and the people in it more so: dirty hair, clothes worn for days on end, faces covered in torturous pick marks, rotting meth mouths, exposed, ravaged arms. I imagined how ill and haunted they would have looked, how needy and desperate they would have smelled. As if death were written on them.

Did they pause and notice the newcomer who looked like he'd just come from a golf course? Maybe. Maybe they had been too focused on their fix to be fazed or interested.

Dutch would have wanted to flee from this place, from a small, smooth stone of a question skipping toward him across the water's surface. *How am I back here?* He would have told himself that he had not been conquered. He had not, like these people, succumbed.

They would have filled him with dread, their proximity threatening infection.

I'd known I would do it the second Glick told me the story. I pulled out my laptop and Googled the raid on the house.

The last time I had done this kind of detective work, I unleashed an avalanche of hits. This time I got only three, two of which were very brief. The third article offered a photo of the raid but only referenced it in a larger story about the opioid epidemic.

I looked at the photo. Cops moved in and out of Jimmy's house. People from inside sat all over the lawn and along the curb, in handcuffs, their heads lowered. The article didn't name them. It focused on people who hadn't known the risk, whose addiction began with injuries.

Like from car accidents.

These people didn't seek out oblivion, like Dutch. Oblivion came to them, the article said, in the form of perfectly legitimate prescriptions from perfectly respectable doctors. Wariness of prescribed medicine hadn't occurred to anyone yet. Painkillers were as readily available as Band-Aids.

Returning to the photo, my eye found the only small daub of bright color in it, a sickly thin woman swimming in a pink hoodie. She was sitting on the curb.

I looked closer. *I know you.*

I didn't really. I knew of her, from a story I'd heard and another newspaper photo I'd seen long ago. A girl on foot.

Dutch had said she was fine. "But she did get banged up."

I leaned in, studying the woman, who was really just a husk of a woman now. *She got more than banged up, Dutch.*

We all had. When we'd stumbled into his light, the impact sent us flying, thrusting us into darkness.

The article described the terrible toll of addiction, not only on the addicts themselves but on their families and friends. One source described how her daughter, once a promising student, had transformed before her very eyes. How their family had become locked in an endless cycle of crisis, rehab, and relapse. How they had learned to expect a phone call reporting her death, how they had drained themselves and their bank accounts trying to save her.

But, the source said, no matter how many overdoses and relapses, no matter how many times their debit cards and valuables went missing, "You never give up. When you love someone, you never give up."

I had never given up. I had always seen Dutch and me as John and June. And we were, I realized now. Just not the set I had envisioned.

Looking at the woman in the photo, I thought of her family, how sure they must have been that her life was just beginning when they had packed her off to college. After the accident, if her parents were like mine, they would have stationed her on their couch and brought her the pills as instructed, along with the remote and extra blankets. After her transformation, did they hold on, like the mother in the article? Did they remain, like June, steadfastly determined and hopeful?

This woman had had friends once, girls who crowded together to take a laughing, smiling picture before a party, girls who would have remained at college and resumed their lives after her injuries sent her home. Maybe initially she'd thought only of her damaged body. But maybe when she'd realized the extent of her loss—her education, her job, her new life and friendships and freedom—maybe then those pills had taken on a life of their own.

She had had a best friend, with whom she had shared matching necklaces, a best friend like Fiona. Maybe, like ours, that friendship had disintegrated as she became unrecognizable.

Once the crackdowns started, pills became so much harder to find, the article said. Some people, people with resources, people like Dutch, could still access them. But after the crackdowns, many turned to heroin. It did the same job, it was cheaper, and it was everywhere.

When I asked Dutch what happened to the girl, he had snapped, "Nothing," hurting me for the first time. He never mentioned her again. The story he had wanted to tell was of how his life was almost ruined. The girl was merely a footnote. Maybe we all were.

Now, the article said, communities across the country strained under the weight of addiction. Not enough intervention services or beds in treatment centers. Not enough first responders to answer the skyrocketing number of overdose calls. Not enough Naloxone. Not enough anything.

The face of the woman in the photo didn't give her away. Her hood and two curtains of limp blond hair obscured it, and with its deterioration, even a full view wouldn't have helped.

Almost nothing of the formerly smiling teenager remained. I leaned toward the photo one more time. At first I thought she was using her hair and hood to hide her face from the camera. I thought she sat angled in this way to accommodate the awkward positioning of her wrists cuffed behind her back. But looking closely, I saw that she was pitched forward, her knees supporting the weight of her torso. Her mouth hung open, jaw slack. She was nodding.

Dutch might not have realized who she was, even if he had caught a glimpse of her in the house. He would have been in such a hurry once he got what he came for. He would have been so relieved to escape that he would not have looked back. With his Ziploc bag itching in his pocket, his mouth watering, his palms sweating, he would have wanted only to be back in the car, barreling away from this place, breathing in his freedom.

And the woman in the picture was so very altered from the girl he and I had seen years before.

Still, I knew her. Looking at her now, I saw her exposed leg where her pant leg had drifted up. I saw a mark I'd seen before, floating between her lower calf and ankle, blurry but discernible. I had never forgotten it, the wobbly hand of an amateur, the zeal of a teen, an attempt at a heart tattoo.

ACKNOWLEDGMENTS

Thanks to Jaynie Royal and the Regal House Publishing team for bringing this book to life.

Thanks to June Carter Cash and the creators of *Walk the Line* for the inspiration, as well as to the American Folklife Center, Library of Congress, for use of "Wildwood Flower."

Some characters and content were originally developed in short stories that appeared in *The Crooked Steeple*. Thanks to KJ Stevens for giving my early work a home.

Thanks to Aaron Boria for your time, expertise, and generosity.

Thanks to Pete Mundt and Lauren Giuliani for all the beautiful photos used to promote this book.

Thanks to my wonderful writing community and to longtime friends Maura Hynes, Tony Bozaan, Brandon Selinsky, Robb Kremer, and Markian Diakiw for supporting me and this project.

Thanks to Taryn Petryk and Christie Prevost, who championed this book from its inception. I would be lost without you.

Thanks to my editor and friend Jason Kirk, who makes me want to be a better writer. This project would never have seen the light of day without your vision and patience.

Thanks to my family, particularly Jack Muldowney, Gael Garbarino Cullen, and my wonderful parents, Rosemary Garbarino and Robert Schikora. I love you.

Book Club Discussion Questions

1. Pink is a recurring color throughout the book. Where does it appear, and what is its significance?

2. The novel depicts three sets of Johnny and June. Where and how do they overlap? Where and how do they diverge?

3. Some characters are never named. What might the author have intended with these omissions?

4. The novel ends without clarifying the fate of the protagonist, Dutch, or their relationship. How do you interpret the ambiguity of the conclusion?

5. Early in the book, Dutch tells the protagonist, "It's one thing to understand, to believe. It's another to actually be different." This sentiment is echoed throughout the book. How do you read the repetition?

Praise for *A Woman in Pink*

"I inhaled this book. Schikora's writing is so sharp and honest, part of you wants to shake her nameless narrator by the shoulders as you would a dear friend. But another, bigger part is sucked fully into her story, which Schikora renders with uncommon empathy and scalpel-sharp details. *A Woman in Pink* manages to be both dazzling and relatable, without a single false note. Anyone who has ever made unwise choices in love, which is to say everybody, should read it immediately."

—Miriam Gershow, author of *Closer* and *Survival Tips: Stories*

"In the middle of Schikora's haunting novel, the unnamed main character looks at herself in the mirror and sees a fragmented, kaleidoscopic image staring back at her in pain. This could well be the singular image that permeates *A Woman in Pink*: the image of the Disease of the Lost Self. Each of Schikora's gut-wrenchingly real characters is suffering from fragmentation and dissociation at various levels. They have become something they no longer recognize, and so, must face the reality of reestablishing a relationship with who they really are. Some begin that universal struggle; others fail to do so. Elegant and concise, this novel is rendered with great ease and confidence and hard-earned insight. A truly graceful and masterful book, it will stay with readers long after the final page is turned."

—Jim Naremore, author of *The Arts of Legerdemain as Taught by Ghosts* and *American Still Life*

"So very true, this story. *A Woman in Pink* is a sharp and sophisticated novel of love and addiction and a certain kind of privilege that devours everything in its path. It's also about friendship and family, the secrets we withhold from those who want what's best for us, and how the ties that bind can keep us afloat, though just as easily, leave us to drown. Schikora's writing is strong and elegant, a salve itself as we weather the blows of a lover who is as vulnerable as he is venomous."

—Laura Scalzo, author of *American Arcadia*

"*A Woman in Pink* had me from page one—a complex, thrilling tale of obsessive love spanning decades, of the role of privilege, the cost of addiction, and how past traumas inform the choices we make, whether we are aware of our predilections or not. What happens when we are so caught up in our own fabrication that we don't realize we are only a footnote in the other person's story? An electrifying debut by a writer to watch."

—Kelly Fordon, author of *Garden for the Blind* and *I Have the Answer*

"The characters in Schikora's *A Woman in Pink* are built with deep emotion and enlivened with blisteringly good dialogue. This is a story of the human heart, every aspect of its complicated motivations and needs, searching to find its way, and Schikora knows how to tell that story with the deft touch of a literary craftsman."

—David W. Berner, author of the Fugere Prize-winning novella *American Moon*

"Much like the sparks that fly from the first moments they meet, *A Woman in Pink* plunges the reader into a compelling relationship between two characters in recovery that blurs the boundaries between love and dependency. Set against the backdrop of the opioid crisis and the privileges of wealth, Schikora's compelling prose vividly unspools the complicated threads of a long-term co-dependent relationship and its consequences. The protagonist's hard-won sense of self in the wake of an eating disorder is challenged when she has to confront both her lover's addiction and the truth behind his role in a tragic accident. As she navigates where redemption ends and enabling begins, the protagonist must reconcile her feminism with the duty of care women are expected to give to family and community, all while battling her own imposter syndrome. *A Woman in Pink* is a smart, suspenseful and wrenching story about learning to let go of the person who was the best worst thing ever to happen."

—Laura Hulthen Thomas, author of *The Meaning of Fear*

"Anyone who's ever been truly in love knows that it's like riding a jet through breathtaking and turbulent skies. But being in love with an addict—well, that's when the jet has lost an engine and the other one is in flames. No other book that I have read has ever described this experience with anything like the vivid emotional accuracy achieved by Megan A. Schikora in her novel, *A Woman in Pink*. She fully inhabits her character's head and so does the reader, who feels acutely—through Schikora's clear, fluid, always believable words—the euphoria of deep connection and caring that gets punctured randomly, over and over, by the shock of letdown, of lies and excuses, of inexplicable anger, and of the fear and pain and self-doubt that become the only constants in a relationship shaped by alcohol and drugs. The immersive flight on which this remarkable book takes a reader through the birth of joy and the dissolution of trust and hope proves intoxicating, in both meanings of the word."

—Carolyn Jack, author of *The Changing of Keys*

"Sometimes bitter, sometimes raw, always revealing and vulnerable, *A Woman in Pink*—told first-person by a main character whose name we never know—exposes how we normalize addictive behavior, how we enable those around us, and ultimately, how we give in and give up to forces that plague us. A beautifully written story about the constant cycle of loss and rediscovery."

—David Haznaw, author of *I Told You I Was Dehydrated*

"Schikora never condescends to her readers, but deftly and subtly encourages them to grasp the vivid truths she exposes. In her raw, yet nuanced description of an addiction—there is more than one kind of addiction, readers will discover—and of the characters who fall into its meshes, readers will be able to understand on a deeper level what is involved in the death-spiral that has impacted so many of our lives. Readers should be prepared to buckle up for an emotional, authentic read that will linger with them long after they close the book."

—Margo Sorenson, author of *Secrets in Translation*

"Addiction is chaos. Instead of focusing on the addict, this incredible story shows the emotional pull and complexity of loving someone in trouble. It will pull you in, making you realize the games addicts play while you remain empathetic to the choices family and loved ones face."

—Marlene F. Byrne, author of *Do Not Discard*

"As readers become witness to the destructive and complex path of those afflicted by addiction—and those who love them—it becomes clear that the central characters are forever locked in an addict tango. Schikora's insightful, resonant, and tragic tale 'of wrath and love' reminds us that when we love, we never give up, even if, or when, behavior signals not only our love's ruin, but our own."

—Deirdre Fagan, author of *Find a Place for Me* and *Phantom Limbs*

"Schikora's *A Woman in Pink* brings into focus the nuances of love and friendship with subtlety and skill. This novel is replete with delightful allusions to classic Americana. Dutch, an alluring but impossible bad boy, is the Johnny Cash to our unnamed protagonist, the *Woman in Pink*'s June Carter. What can we do when the feeling of love is attainable but the people we love are not? 'You can't love a bad man,' her mother insists. The redemptive element that shines out amidst this existential quandary is the radical empathy of female friendship and the stern but loving counsel that it can generate. Schikora examines the bad-boy trope without falling into its trappings. In the end, *A Woman in Pink* isn't choosing between two different men, she's choosing herself."

—Sarah Pazur, author of "The Little Tramp," *TriQuarterly*